AF556050

THIRTY ONE

PANDEMIC LETTERS OF LOSS & LOVE

New Delhi to / from New York

THIRTY ONE

PANDEMIC LETTERS OF LOSS & LOVE

New Delhi to / from New York

Bijayalaxmi Nanda
and
Sangita Misra

HAR-ANAND
PUBLICATIONS PVT LTD

HAR-ANAND PUBLICATIONS PVT LTD
E-49/3, Okhla Industrial Area, Phase-II, New Delhi-110020
Tel.: 41603490
E-mail: info@haranandbooks.com/haranand@rediffmail.com
Shop online at: www.haranandbooks.com

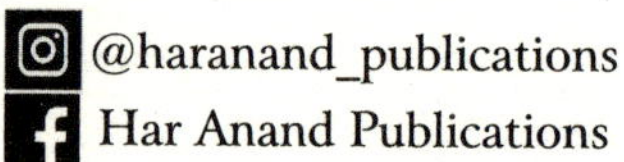

Cover and illustration design by Rajesh Singh

Published by Ashok Gosain and Ashish Gosain for
Har-Anand Publications Pvt Ltd

Printed in India at Yash Printographics

Dedicated to

To my mother Manorama, my aunt Durgesh Nandini, my mothers-in-law Munni and Radhika and my friend Mitu, who I will continue to write to with my prayers.

– Bijayalaxmi Nanda

To my mother Dr. Binapani Satpathy and my father Dr. Naba Kishore Satpathy.

– Sangita Misra

Endorsements

A profound and delightful read on friendship between women which reinvigorates and evokes joy and hope.

– Prof. Rajni Abbi
Professor, Faculty of Law
University of Delhi

This collection of letters in the setting of the covid speaks of the magical power of friendship between women which is transformative in every sense.

– Prof. Neera Agnimitra
Professor
Department of Social Work, University of Delhi

What would we be without the friendships that sustain us? This was especially true during the horrible Covid times where a surreal reality engulfed everyone's lives. In a sensitive book that intertwines the personal and political Dr Bijayalaxmi Nanda and her friend Sangita captures this poignant reality between two friends separated now by decades & continents but united by common universal values of love & loss. And it's the ultimate celebration of friendship.

– Chandni Ahlawat Dabas
Noted Film & Television Producer

Thirty One Pandemic Letters is at once a poignant and at the same time a heart-warming book. When the current pandemic's restrictions caused, at first, their homes to be transformed from sanctuary to gloomy confinement, the authors rekindled a childhood friendship across continents by writing to each other. The process was clearly cathartic and uplifted their spirits in these tough times that take an emotional toll. Dealing with their lives as professionals, as well as personal responsibilities, these letters are full of courage, hope, joy and the essence of connecting as human beings. It makes an engrossing, delightful read.

– Baijayant 'Jay' Panda

Member of Parliament
and Author

An ode to the strength of friendship and energy of the art of writing, which connects in a way that heals the mind and soul. In times of this Pandemic, which is something that has isolated us, "31 Pandemic letters" provides a deeper understanding of how women go through the trials and tribulations of daily life and how seeking solace in the words of one another helps keep misery at bay and dissolves the feeling of loneliness. The frank exchange of stories of life in this Pandemic from two different parts of the world, makes you think how we are all similar in a way. In this world of social media and short texts we have forgotten how long letters and emails help convey true emotions and feelings.

– Nila Madhab Panda

Film-maker

Thirty one Pandemic Letters is like a whiff of fresh air in the stifling restrictions of the pandemic ... reaching out to friends via letters and establishing bonds sends out a reassuring message of hope and light amidst the darkness of confinement.

I wish her all success.

– Dr Baijayanti Mishra

Writer and
Sahitya Academy Awardee

Alone

"Lying, thinking
Last night
How to find my soul a home
Where water is not thirsty
And bread loaf is not stone
I came up with one thing
And I don't believe I'm wrong
That nobody,
But nobody
Can make it out here alone."

– Maya Angelou

So don't be frightened, dear friend, if a sadness confronts you larger than any you have ever known, casting its shadow over all you do. You must think that something is happening within you, and remember that life has not forgotten you; it holds you in its hands and will not let you fall. Why would you want to exclude from your life any uneasiness, any pain, any depression, since you don't know what work they are accomplishing within you?

– Rainer Maria Rilke,
Letters to a Young Poet

Contents

	Foreword	13
	Acknowledgments	19
	Prologue	27
	Introduction	33
	Illustrator's Note	41
	Glossary	45
	Family Tree	46
I	The Beginning	47
II	A Lockdown within a Lockdown	52
III	The Karmic Zoom	54
IV	Masquerades	58
V	Sand Mirrors	61
VI	Pink Rage	64
VII	Common Cold Gone Rogue	68
VIII	Living in Harmony	71
IX	Red Coat in Times Square	74
X	Of Chirping Birds and the Past	76
XI	Between a Rock and a Hard Place	79
XII	Reading Dostoevsky in Corona Times	83
XIII	Dying in the Arms of Trees	85
XIV	Kabuliwallah and Summer Stories	89
XV	Memories of Incandescent Ice	93
XVI	Samba Dance and Herbal Cures	97
XVII	Dalai Lama and Fred Rogers	100
XVIII	Affection, Addiction and Cinco de Mayo	103

XIX	The Immigrant Bride	107
XX	Of Meera Bai and the Short Tresses	110
XXI	Rabindranath Tagore and the Offer of Songs	113
XXII	Ferdinand and Gitanjali	117
XXIII	Being Poor	124
XXIV	New Delhi and Old York	126
XXV	Aurobindo and Eternity of Soul	134
XXVI	Breathless in the Hybrid of Networks	137
XXVII	Phantom and the Colour of Beauty	140
XXVIII	Monali's Departure	145
XXIX	Distance and Dreams	149
XXX	Achilles Heel	151
XXXI	The Intermission of Compensatory Memory	153
	Epilogue	156
	Appendix – Recipes of loss and love	163

Foreword-1

FIGHTING COVID-19 BY LETTER WRITING

Letter writing, once upon a time, was considered as an important branch of creative Literature, at par with classics. One good example of this is the modern classic "Glimpses of World History" that consisted of 196 letters of Jawaharlal Nehru to his young daughter Indira, in the year 1934. This book was considered later as a panoramic history of humankind that had set a record as a unique way of writing history through epistolary style borrowed from the tradition of belles letters.

These letters of Nehru were written from different locations of the British Prison Houses in India where he was interned during the Freedom Movement of India, against the Imperial British rule, in the last Century. These invaluable letters Nehru wrote were not mere homilies that usually parents write to their children at home, from abroad. These letters were subsequently collected together and were published as an important literary work that reinterpreted World history from an Asia-centric view point of judgement of historiography against the dominant colonial Eurocentric way of writing history that is still in vogue today.

In the above context here is another book titled, "Pandemic Letters" that is going to be published soon. This book consists of 31 letters that were exchanged through E-Mails, between two friends, living far away from each other, in two opposite sides of the globe; one in New York and the other in New Delhi, during the ensuing Covid 19 Pandemic that had cast its spell all over the world, paralysing human activities while shutting down the world, as a whole, into a global prison house!

The writers of this interesting epistolary are two erstwhile school mates, Bijayalaxmi Nanda and Sangita Misra. They hail from Odisha where they cultivated friendship during their schooling years in Cuttack. Their friendship continued to prosper even after they grew up and entered into their own pursuits of life and livelihood in different places of the world, through their respective professional careers. After forty years, since their friendship flourished at the school in India, Sangita now in her fifties, is at present living in New York City and her friend Bijayalaxmi in New Delhi, holding on to their respective professional occupations.

In spite of physical separation the two friends continued to maintain their friendship in normal ways of communication over telephone when Corona Pandemic struck and the world came to a grinding halt all of a sudden. With physical movements restricted to the four walls of the home the two friends got alerted and knew that a time has come when human civilization is being challenged by some unwholesome force of Dark Nature that must be resisted by a determined will power of the civilised human world by all means! And that led to exchanges of thoughts between both friends, two enlightened minds, through writing letters over e-mails resulting in the present book!

Since letter writing, as an Art form, is slowly getting extinct in the modern world of Information Technology the present book "Pandemic Letters", by the authors is expected to serve as a land mark in the annals of epistolary literature in posterity.

With blessings.

Professor Santanu Kumar Acharya

M.Sc. D.Litt.

Renowned Academician and

Academy Award Winning Novelist and Story Writer, India

Foreword-2

"This is my letter to the World
That never wrote to Me-
The simple News that Nature told
With tender Majesty"

In early nineteenth century when Emily Dickinson underlined herself as a " chitti rasa", a conduit of Nature who writes on her behalf to the world that doesn't care to write back, little did she know that in the remote corners of Colonial India the newly opened girls' school were actually aiming to introduce courses which could teach them (a) simple maths for maintaining a good budget at home (running the household in the limited means) and (b) writing letters to the "pardesi piyas" posted somewhere in Calcutta, Madras, Rangoon or one of those tea-estates in Assam where they usually took a mistress. In one of the famous poems by Trilochan, Champa, an eight year old girl of a milkman, as talkative as Mini in Kabuliwala or Muneeza in Faiz's poem" Ik wahi hain hamari dictator," gives a damn to the poet's proposal of educating herself. When he tells her, "Gandhi Baba ki iccha hai/sab jan padhna-likhna seekhen" and also points towards the fact that this will enable her to write letters to her future husband posted somewhere in Kalkutta, immediately this chatter box blurts out"

"If ever I take a husband/I shall not let him go anywhere/And to hell with Kalkutta"(Kalkutte par bajar gire")

Bijaylaxmi and her friend Sangita too were born in the erstwhile "Province of Bengal" but by the time she started going to school, the objective of women's education had changed considerably. Outspoken Champas had grown into intelligent and accomplished girls like Bijaya and her friend posted abroad to whom she has written these letters with such elan and grace on pertinent issues during Covid stress. This voyage from the stage of being little "baby women" to that of walking tall as full-fledged thinking women and responsible citizens of the world can very well be traced in the correspondence bridging hearts and minds together in two cultural contexts.

Sweet are the uses of adversity. Even calamity has a silver lining to it: it underlines the oneness of beings across the world: wars, natural disasters and pandemics of all sorts are also a blow to the bloated human ego in the sense that they go all out to prove what Blake propounded almost two hundred years ago: " We are to God what flies are to a wanton boy/ He kills us for his sport "

As school girls Bijayalaxmi and Sangita would have definitely played the game of Statue together. Covid too played Statue with us, arresting our movements, freezing us wherever we were. But challenges are opportunities too, and this book of intimate chit chat between old friends on issues great and small is a case in point.

Anamika

Renowned Professor in English

and Academy Award Winning Bilingual Poet and Novelist, India

Foreword-3

दु:ख सबको माँजता है – अज्ञेय

कोविड मनुष्य की चुनौतियों की अग्निपरीक्षा थी। इसने मानवीय सम्वेदनाओं को झकझोर कर सृजनात्मक रूप में अभिव्यक्ति का अवसर भी दिया। पान्डेमिक लेटर्स देश, काल और हृदय की दूरियों को पारकर मानवीय संवेदनाओं की यात्रा की वह अनुभूति है, जिसमें कोविड काल में भारतीय परिप्रेक्ष्य में नारी जीवन के अनुभवों, उनकी संवेदना एवं मित्रता के कालजयी भाव को बेहद प्रभावी एवं सशक्त रूप में अभिव्यक्त किया गया है।

अतीव मानवीय गुणों से समृद्ध प्रो. बिजयलक्ष्मी नंदा एवं संगीता मिश्रा दोनों ही अकादमिक दक्षता और श्रेष्ठता के भी अप्रतिम उदाहरण हैं। पान्डेमिक लेटर्स में इनके भावों की तरल और निर्दोष अभिव्यक्ति आकर लेती है।

- चित्रा मुदगल

उपन्यासकार,लेखक

Acknowledgement-1

This book took us four long years to publish; therefore, my list of acknowledgments is very extensive. It includes all those whom I lost in the past four years and all the love that surrounds me. I am deeply grateful to Narendra Kumar of Har-Anand Publications, a doyen of Indian Publishing and a friend, philosopher, guide, and mentor who encouraged me to publish the letters. His presence in my life is heightened by his absence now that this book is on its way to publication. Gratitude in every way to him and his sons Ashish and Ashok Gosain, who retrieved this project and patiently helped me move forward on it.

Special thanks to Kamala Bhasin, whose life and teachings I draw inspiration from, and who taught me about the eternal bonds of friendship between women. My brother-in-law Sunandan would have celebrated this publication with utmost joy. I miss his presence in my life.

I am indebted to Santanu Acharya, Anamika and Chitra Mudgal, well-known writers and Sahitya Academy awardees, for their patience and grace in writing the forewords for us. Gratitude to Prof. Rajni Abbi and Prof. Neera Agnimitra for endorsing the work. I have learned from them the strength and support we derive from women's friendship. Thanks to Prof. Malashri Lal, Abhay K., Baijayant, Jay Panda, Chandni Ahlawat Dabas, Baijyanti Mishra, and others for their kind words of endorsement.

I would like to acknowledge the love that surrounds me in my work family at Miranda House – Mallika Verma, Nisha Vashista, Nandini Dutta, Amrita T. Sheikh, Purnima Roy, Jayashree Pillai, Subha, Namrata Singh, Shruti Sharma, Monika Tomar, Monika Vij, Bashabi Gupta, and all other colleagues who did their work so ably and efficiently that I found some stolen leisure time to pursue this writing. A special thanks to Hena Singh for her constant help and support.

My acknowledgment extends to the friendships of women that sustained me throughout my life – childhood friends Gayatri Mishra (dearest heart), Sujata Patnaik, Pragyan Chaudhury, Usha Rani, M. Sheela, Renu, Swetleena, and friends found in this lifetime – Shashi Motilal, Debra Nicholson, Suman, Chirashree Ghosh, Krishna Menon, Nonica Datta, Rakhee Bakshee, and Lotty Alaric. Beyond the terrain of friendships of my tribe of strong, powerful, generous, beautiful women, there are a few good men too – Ajay Dhawan, Kali Mahapatra, D.P., Pritish and K.M. Tata who encouraged me to write. Then the love of a chosen family of my heart and soul – Eisha Roy (God-Daughter and motivator), Nupur Ray, Sharmistha Mahapatra, Amrita Sathpathy, Arushi Patnaik (Soul Sisters), Wagner and Santu (sons of my heart) whose support is immense. Daughter of my heart – Shelly Jeena, surrounded me with love, patience, care, and diligently worked on this manuscript, adding to it in every way that she could. Sunita Malkani for her editing of first draft.

I owe a special thanks to Dushyant Kumar for being my very first reader and patiently providing me with inputs. Thanks are due to Supriya and Manish too for engaging with this work. My sisters – Upali and Aptakami – are my conscientious critics, and my sisters-in-law, my loving admirers – Seema, Nita, Sunita, Archana, and Vandana. My nieces Tanu, Lavanya, Ritwika, Ria, Akankhsha, Muskan, Sanjana, Soham, Ashita and Pihu have always engaged with me in every way and enriched my writing.

Thanks are due to my cousins, especially Soumyakant for his wisdom, Menu, Promod, Chandra, Shiv, Surya, Jigisha, Prajit, Nikita and my brothers-in-love – Sachin, Niraj, Ravi, Niraj, Sanjay, and Shankar. My nephews Adarsh, Omy, Ansh and Nishant and nephews-in-love Dhruv, and Madhur. My aunts – Taru, Rita, Lily and Charu – for their affection and constant belief that I can go on this path of writing.

I am grateful to my daughter Akshara for being my conscience keeper, for incisive comments on my work, for discussions on writing and writers, and for being a window to the world of diverse literature and her own wondrous expressions. Gratitude to her for bearing with all my madness.

I am indebted to my father Amulya Ratna Nanda for many discussions and for enriching each and every phase of my evolution and growth. In our intermediate years, he tutored Sangita and me in English Literature. It is that tutoring that has borne fruit! My spouse Rajesh is the genius illustrator of this work. Clearly, he is my fellow traveler in every sense, and his support is the reason these letters get such magical wings. So gratitude to him in every way.

Finally, to Sangita, who bore my procrastination with publishing this work with the patience of a Himalayan Yogi. The biggest blow to me was when her father passed away during this period; he was very keen to see our work. It broke my heart for disappointing him by my delay. But Sangita never held it against me. Friendships can sustain for eternity only if we accept each other with all our flaws and with deep patience and forgive each other every day. She taught me that with her compassion.

To all those I have not mentioned, you know who you are. Thank you for believing that words can heal.

Bijayalaxmi Nanda

Acknowledgement-2

Thanks to Har-Anand Publications, Narendra Kumar and his sons Ashish and Ashok Gosain. Grateful to Santanu Acharya and Anamika for engaging with the work and writing the foreword, and all endorsement note writers for their encouragement. Special thanks to Rajesh for amazing illustrations and the cover page and Baijayant 'Jay' Panda for his kind words.

Thanks to my grandparents Prof. Ghanshyam Dash, Smt. Bisakha Dash, Mr. Bata Krushna Satpathy and especially my paternal grandmother, Smt. Hemalata Satpathy, whose poetic genes run in my vein.

Thanks to my father, Dr. N.K Satpathy, for initiating me into the "Khadi Chuan" (Touching the chalk on a slate). In 1971, I wrote on a slate, with a very thick chalk, initiated by my father. He held my fingers firmly with his and we drew three circles, representing Brahma, Vishnu and Maheshwara. He taught me to write the first alphabets and words.

My mother Dr. Binapani Satpathy, for instilling in me the love of writing and providing constant encouragement to pursue creative writing seriously.

My brother Er. Bijoy Kumar Satapathy, for his subtle encouragement to think on a higher philosophical plane.

My English tutor during high school, Ms. Mullah, who taught me the craft of writing essays in English, and developing the skill of quirky thinking, Professor Patricia Hickey in Nursing School, who encouraged me to pursue creative writing. My husband Dr. Sameer K. Misra, for his subtle sarcasm and constructive criticism that challenged me to pen down my thoughts.

My inlaws Dr. Somnath Misra and Smt. Susama Misra, for teaching the art of not falling prey to procrastination.

My children Soumya, Satwick and Sachin, who always encouraged me to think on their level and experiment with imaginative writing. Their interesting queries to test their mother's psyche, has led me into many interesting journeys into the foray of writing.

My sincere thanks to my friends Ms. Emilia Vrabie, Dr Nibedita Mohanty, Dr. Sangeeta Mohanty, Mr. Satyajit Mishra, Justice. Savitri Ratho,and Ms.Vicki Bogard who encouraged and motivated me to keep writing and reach for the moon.

My family members, Prof. Rajlakshmi Mishra, Mrs. Anupama Dash, Dr. Kamala Nanda, Mrs. Pramila Satpathy, Ms. Nivedita Ganapathi, Dr. Gayatri Mohapatra, Ms. Jayshree Nanda, Ms. Bhagyashree Mishra/Satpathy, Mr. Sanjoy Satpathy, Mrs Priyadarshini Satpathy Ms. Rene Shanker, Ms. Nanda Shanker, Mrs. Suvarna Mishra and Dr. Baijayanti Mishra, who patiently read my poetry and short stories and gave their honest input.

My special thanks to Mr. Santanu Nandy, who stood by me through thick and thin , carrying my departed father on his shoulders, standing like a pillar of strength, in the cemetery where my father turned into fire, smoke, and ether and merged into the universe. They say, the one who stands by you on a cemetery ground, is the one you must keep closest to your soul.

A special shout out to '83 Sisters, my batchmates from St Joseph's Convent Girls High School, Cuttack, who have been a constant source of strength and inspiration.

My sincere thanks to Mr. Pranab Kar, who keeps motivating me to write and publish my musings.

Thanks to my colleagues from NYC DOHMH and DOE who enabled me to aspire for more. My deepest gratitude of having had the privilege of working as the reference librarian in Business, Science and Technology and Senior Children's Librarian in the Central Library of Queen's Public Library, which furthered my interest in writing for posterity.

Thanks to all my family and friends, whose name maybe missing here but have been a profound part of my life energy.

Lastly, my sincere thanks to my childhood friend, philosopher and soul sister, of forty four years Dr. Bijayalaxmi Nanda who started this journey for us by reaching out to me with an email in March 2020. *Thirty One Pandemic Letters* would not have come into fruition without her.

Sangita Misra

Prologue-1

Thirty-one Pandemic Letters of Loss and Love: New Delhi to New York

I started writing because it was the only way I could get on to the next day. The only way the day was bearable. The cruel sunlight burnt into my skin peeling it away to expose me to the mercy of winter's chaffing winds. There was an unbearable pain I bore in my childhood bones which screamed in the night to tell me their story. I did not belong to the world around me of hyperactive children who bounced around like colourful balloons in a dazzling spring sky. I wrote to make sense of it all ... of pain and loss, of isolation and alienation. I wrote in secrecy about the adults who pried on children and caught them in their intricate butterfly nets. I wrote in secrecy of the imploding stars in the sky and of my transparent pubescent body trying to hold the stars in them. Numbers made no sense to me. They jumped off the school blackboard to mock me with their unfathomability. Written words stitched skilfully by great writers came to my rescue. They were my thicketed shade from the blazing sunlight, the balm to my crying bones and the warm cover for my vulnerable transparent body. Books are a girl's best friend was not just a grand saying for me. It was my pathetic truth. I had friends but none I held close to speak my heart to. There is a certain naivety and brashness in children which makes them merciless. They pick on the weak, the different, the unusual and the unique. The innocence of children so celebrated in so many ways is a half-truth. Some children scar other children for life. And all adults are not the protectors of childhood. Some adults destroy your childhood for life. At thirteen years I knew enough to age me a hundred years.

My father's government service ensured that we travelled from place to place. Each home had its corner for my secrets. I wrote feverishly on sand and bricks and tree trunks. My secrets were dangerous enough to unsettle the secure home I inhabited. My mother's beauteous smile and principled ways, my father's soft presence and gentle composure, my sweet sisters' gossamer wings had to be protected at any cost. So I wrote my secrets on crumpled papers and threw them to the wind. Little girls hide enormous secrets in the folds of their beautifully tailored pleated skirts. They are taught to do that to keep peace. It is a huge burden to be a little girl sometimes. I wrote to lighten that burden.

I met Sangita when I was thirteen and I read genuine acceptance in her eyes. She saw me with my crooked, twisted bones, my peeling skin, my cowering gaping self. She saw me broken and yet found me whole. There was no mocking gaze or rejection. Acceptance changes everything. I felt I could tell her my secrets. I felt lighter by her side. Finally, a best friend beyond my dog eared copy of Louisa May Alcott's Little Women or Jane Austen's Pride and Prejudice. a mirror to reflect my transparency. My words found a nest beyond my secret scribbles. All those words said to her were not always my unsaid ones. For words once spoken are difficult to erase. However, much was said between us healing me in ways beyond Sangita's own comprehension.

In 1980s I lost my maternal aunt who was only twenty-eight years to cancer. She was my most favourite adult and she did proclaim that I was her most favourite child. She was like a thick bower of vibrant spring flowers. She made you feel loved by just saying your name. I was not a child to her to be ticked or reprimanded but a person with important ideas and valuable judgements. She was a very precious part of my world and she died leaving a deep void in my life. My writing returned to claim me now more publicly. I wrote angsty poetry in fragments here and there. Some got published in school magazines and were forgotten in the natural order of things. Romantic poems replaced them as I grew older. Sometimes a short story would be born in a kernel of my mind and I would engage my friends with my story telling. In Bhubaneswar, Odisha where I lived a large part of my teenage years one summer vacation I initiated a magazine with a group of friends and my sisters. These were my tiny adventurous forays into a writing world.

Then in July 1990 my mother died within six months of her cancer being diagnosed. She was in her early forties and had a certain robust disposition and a natural claim to permanency in every sense. So her death was akin to the nuclear bombing of Hiroshima and Nagasaki in Japan during the Second World War. Everything that I held dear was blown to smithereens. It was not just the immediate damage of losing a parent but its impact like a nuclear explosion is felt even today. My writing returned in a feverish wave to mend my fragmented self. Short stories of loss, longing and life intermeshed. My mother's illness coincided with my father moving to New Delhi for his posting. With her death in Delhi the sense of losing my roots from my home state Odisha seeped in slowly and surely. The language in Delhi was alien in many ways and so was the culture. I wrote many poems and short stories during this period talking about alienation and loss. Most were stories of women who could not belong or were discriminated. A few got published too. One found its way to the *Femina* magazine. I started working as a teacher in a Women's College ie Miranda House in Delhi. I taught Political Science and was essentially drawn to ideas of gender equality and rights. The college exposed me to the world of feminist writings and readings, to phenomenal women who lent their voices to the cause of women. Miranda House in many ways is like Begum Rokeya's novella 'Sultana's Dream' ... a feminist utopia.

My writing took a different turn with the wings of my activism and academics. Some articles and books were written and published as part of the rituals of the academic community. A manuscript of my collection of poems titled Mothers and Daughters is languishing on my desk for last five years or more. A collection of short stories is also vying for attention. Some of my stories made their way into screenplays too. But I shunned away from owning them completely. Somehow the ritual of publication seems arduous to me. My writing is an expression as well as a process to heal. My energies dissipate when the process of publication begins. I need to be motivated about it all the time. My poems received a lot of encouragement from friends who are writers – the most precious is that of Kamla Bhasin. Kamladi as we lovingly called her in fact translated one of my English poems into Hindi giving it widespread publicity on social media! It did fill my heart with joy and purpose.

The Pandemic of Covid-19 and the subsequent global lockdown coincided with the premature death of a dear fellow traveller, It led to a deep vacuum in me. A pandemic of grief overpowered me. Mitu and I met due to our joint quest for gender justice. Her story is now well known as that of a woman who fought against her in-laws and her husband to save the lives of her twin daughters. In a country which continues to prefer sons and regards daughters as liabilities her story reverberates with many. However, the fact that she could not be forced for sex-selective abortion, gave birth to her daughters and fought a long legal battle with her husband made her a hero in every sense. Her premature death in March 2020 broke my spirits. Death is the ultimate separation. It tears every vestige of hope and courage. We strive to cope ... to move forward but it is indeed tough. My email exchanges with my dearest friend Sangita came to my rescue. Friendships between women and the bonds it creates are lifesaving in many ways. Sangita's friendship appeared again in my life to nurture and restore my spirits. She feels I restored hers. This is the beauty of our belongingness. This is our first joint venture into creative writing. I hope you will enjoy reading our letters.

– Bijayalaxmi Nanda
August 21, 2020

Prologue-2

My mother asked me to write. I asked "How?" She replied calmly "with a pen on paper." I questioned "what?" "Anything," she said. "What does that mean?" was my cheeky question. "Anything that comes to your mind, take a pen, take a piece of paper and start writing." The following day she gifted me with a diary. It had a navy blue resin cover and the year on it was 1979. "Start today" she said. "Writing will open up your mind and make you a better person." "In what way?" I queried. "In ways you will never dream of, your diary will be your best friend and connect you to your feelings and emotions and will not judge your thoughts or emotions. You can fall back on it and reflect upon your words and grow from it." I maintained a diary through the course of my teenage years in India and Iraq, where my parents had gone on an assignment to teach in Basrah Medical College. My diary and I became inseparable and I carried it wherever I went.

On a train journey in India from the East to the North, my knapsack was robbed during an overnight journey. Along with it, all my childhood memories were stolen by an unknown thief; the night thief took my most prized belonging – my navy blue, resin clothed diary. The shock of being robbed of my childhood memories was devastating. I stopped writing altogether.

My perceptive mother then, introduced me to the concept of penpals. She suggested I start writing to 'friends' from all over the globe- they were people, similar to my age, whom I never met before, or would ever meet, to communicate with them through writing letters. "What is the point of this?" I lashed out. "It will open up your horizon of thinking and dreaming. You will make friends with strangers and see the world through their eyes and gather unique perspectives about life, you would have never dreamed before." Thus began a new phase of writing for me. My pen friends hailed from Morocco, Libya, Britain and Jamaica. It was a thrilling experience to write and receive letters from them. It broadened my knowledge of different continents and their culture and traditions. Slowly I grew out of this, although the habit of writing letters stayed with me and kept me connected with my parents, relatives and beloved friends, when I left India and migrated into an alien land in 1991.

Innumerable letters sustained my lonesome existence in a land that I adopted as home. My mother gave me the most precious gift; the gift of penning down my thoughts in happy times and sad times; in critical periods of time when the crisis close at hand seemed insurmountable.

Thirty years have passed by in New York, I still continue to dabble in writing letters – paper and pen have been replaced by naked fingers tapping on a keyboard. The world has become tiny compared to the world that I lived in, where pen friends existed, and my mother was around me in the physical realm. The flame that she had lit within me continues to burn.

It is during this COVID -19 crisis, I reached out to my dearest childhood friend Bijayalaxmi, like I would have reached out to my resin clothed navy blue diary and poured my thoughts into her. She soaked it all up and showered me back with her healing words to reflect upon as well.

Thirty-One Pandemic Letters thus composed itself by becoming an amalgamation of two streams of letters merging together and becoming an elixir of life.

– Sangita Misra
August 19, 2020

Introduction-1

The Beginning

It was the usual harried day at work in my comparatively recent assignment as Principal of Miranda House, a college in the University of Delhi, India where I have been teaching for last twenty-seven years. Files sitting patiently on each other in their pink and yellow covers, my pen poised in the air in my unpractised hand for an uncertain tremulous signature for the papers to be finally on their journey to another desk ... the usual story of life's work rituals. Newspapers on our doorsteps and articles now circulating on the internet had alerted all of us here to the impending arrival of a dangerous' epidemic' Covid 19. The stories from Wuhan, China, many cities of Italy and Iran were bone chilling. The symptoms of a common cold deadly enough to snuff out lives in a short span and the spread possible through just a mild touch or presence. A tall bottle of hand sanitiser had already made its way to all our office desks. We also prepared a Covid19 preparedness response for the office training the staff on social distancing and the like. It was a short spring break at work. Except for me and the administrative staff, the college was empty. The faculty members and students were away. It seemed surreal in every way.

I tried to convince myself that like the earlier epidemic SARs or H1N1 this phase will also ebb away. The World Health Organisation (WHO) was still calling it an epidemic. Two weeks is how long it will last is how I perceived it in the beginning. I whispered to myself "when students come back we can maintain sanitiser dispensers everywhere ... and provide a protocol and all will be fine". But there was a niggling doubt in my head as if by sixth sense that this time this epidemic was different. This time there was a feeling of foreboding in the air. of a massive overhaul. of something so deadly that we would have no control over it ... that life as we know it till now was going to change drastically ... but I had no living experience to imagine the tumultuous change... It was early March 2020. Spring flowers bloomed unheralded all around the exquisite red brick building that is my workplace. The fragrance of the petunias, the dahlias, the chrysanthemum and their multi-hued rainbow colours spoke only of good health and exuberant cheer. The news of the epidemic spreading like wildfire seemed an absolute contrast to the ambience around.

It was March 11, 2020. The WHO announced the Covid19 as a pandemic. A pandemic after a hundred years ... the sceptre of the Spanish flu loomed large. Death and stigma both join hands in a pandemic. it robs you away of comfort and dignity. For all of us the immediacy was what kept us on tenterhooks. I was in charge of holding a whole institution together. I felt overwhelmed. Was I capable of rising to this occasion? How can I manage to hold all of it together? Such questions buzzed around in my head making me feel isolated and vulnerable. I felt I was in Dante's Inferno ... entering a hell of earth's own making. Perhaps even my own making ... words from the Inferno reflected my plight "All hope abandon ye who enter here". Like Dante in the inferno I was seized by terror and slowly and steadily falling into a paralysed trance.

There were still around a hundred students staying in the hostel of the college who had not returned home for the spring break. It became my first concern their safety was paramount. The safety of the staff who came to college was important. My father was seventy-eight years and a cancer survivor... I also had to take care of things at home so that he did not fall sick. My daughter was in New York studying for her masters. She was to be with us in the summer vacations. Now New York was severely impacted. I felt a deep sense of separation from her suddenly. a separation from my own identity as her mother. I no longer would be able to protect her or reach out to her. she was now truly on her own. Both my professional and personal crisis amalgamated and a pandemic of fears took hold of my mind.

The mind is the most powerful as well as the most vulnerable when it comes to our health both physical as well as mental. It can orchestrate its own world and bind us in it. I felt trapped and claustrophobic.

By 24 March 2020 the Government announced a nation-wide lockdown for the greater good of combating the pandemic. Social distancing, wearing of masks, use of hand sanitisers, online classes for students became new buzzwords. I stopped going to work. A suitable area of my dining table became my designated work desk. In a couple of days, I spent ten hours or more on that desk working on my laptop through various online platforms including Zoom, Google and CISCO Webex. a network of artificial connections where we are all reduced to a unidimensional talking pictures, interacting on a regular basis as if this is the way to be.

Our part-time house helps were also unable to come because of the lockdown and the domestic chores of the home were added to my duties. We tried a fair division between me, my spouse and my father striving to maintain equality in every sense. Our mediocre skills in the domestic arena were managed by our ability to not be concerned about perfect housekeeping. Odisha's culinary wonders which are mostly boiled and mashed vegetables, plain rice and curd preparations came to my absolute rescue. However, the balancing act made me tired and listless. I lost a dear friend during this period and it hit me hard. Her presence was like that of a luminescent candle. She lit up my life in my deepest and darkest moments. I could not even attend her funeral due to the lockdown situation. I did not even know how to mourn her. How do you mourn the death of someone you believed was permanent? How do you extinguish the hope that makes living possible…? The ephemerality of this existence made me insecure and I struggled with a despair for which I could find no answers. Every morning I woke up broken and every day I put myself together. Any word of comfort offered seemed factitious. The depth of life is measured by the emotive connections we make. Work can never be enough for us. It cannot fill the empty spaces in our lives. It cannot replace the joys and pleasures of friendships, interacting with family members and loved ones. I found comfort in speaking to childhood friends and reminiscing about our time together. I could be myself with them, imperfect, flawed and broken and they found nothing wrong with it. There were no pretences with them. It was the perfect emotional retreat.

It is in the process of writing messages to my childhood best friend Sangita that this collection came to being. Sangita and I have been friends for four decades. We met when we were thirteen and continued this relationship like a flowing river of companionable silence and speech. It is a miraculous friendship sustained by truth and forgiveness. My letters (through emails) to Sangita saved me, they rescued me from spinning into a never ending tunnel of pain. So it was not a knight in shining armour nor a romantic love of my life that saved me from the throes of my pain. But the opening of my heart to a female friend and the complete faith that I will be affirmed and validated.

The letters are quirky, full of our everyday life experiences and also the stories of cities with lives of their own. Cuttack, in Odisha India where we met for the first time. My father was posted in the city and we were living in a government bungalow located near the Mahanadi river and around the ruins of the 13th century Barabati Fort. The fort was built by King Anangabhimadeva of the Ganga dynasty. The ruins that remain include the gate of the fort, moat around it and a mound which archaeological studies say is the nine storied palace of the king. This rich history spun a fairy-tale quality around our adolescent years. Sangita was my neighbour then staying with her uncle and aunt in a government quarter adjacent to ours. We studied in separate schools but spent our evenings together walking around the moat or sitting on our favourite rock jutting into the swampy moat. It was an idyllic time. Then life's energies finally brought us to Delhi and New York respectively and every time we met we made it a ritual to recreate our childhood times. So Cuttack, New Delhi and New York are the reverberating cities in the background of the letters with a life of their own reflecting their specific cultures, cuisines, candour and catharsis.

This is an ode to bonds between women proving the soul sustaining strength that friendships provide, this is an exploration of Pandemic times which leaves us with very little to depend on except our own strengths drawn from people who care for us, this is also to provide the reader with an in-depth understanding of the way in which women negotiate their lives and grapple with decisions and support each other from descending into misery. This is a celebration of female bonds during one of the most difficult periods of contemporary history.

In the Bell Jar Sylvia Plath's exquisite novel about how a woman finds herself spiralling into depression because society has no place for women's aspirations there is a sentence about the pain of deep despair the protagonist Esther Greenwood says and I quote "to the person in the bell jar blank and stopped as a dead baby, the world is a bad dream" So I think to myself "If the world is a bad dream how do we escape it? Our letters to each other, Thirty-one of them that we share here as representative of a full blossoming month in a Gregorian calendar but actually spanning four months in this period. The thirty-one letters speak of a complete cycle. It is our offering to the world to dispel myths about female friendships which are stereotypically constructed as full of envy, jealousy and cruelty. It is this swirly tenderness between us that made us survive. All I can say for myself is my best friend through her letters saved me from a pandemic. She was my Covid19 healer. We all need a little earth, a sliver of sunshine and a drizzle of rain for hope to be born. Sangita my dearest me provided me with all that and much more. I hope our correspondence with each other uplifts your spirits, gives you comfort in your difficult times and gives sustenance to your soul. I hope it inspires you to celebrate your female friends and recognise their significant role in your life. I have become sensitive about the magical power of female friendships learning from my dearest friend, philosopher and guide Kamla Bhasin. Her commitment to gender equality is poised on the wings of trust, friendship and love. She has strengthened my belief in the power.

Here's to female friendships, here's to life and hope! May we emerge more empathetic and supportive from the pandemic to each other. Here's to inspiring women ... grandmothers, mothers, sisters, friends and daughters, may their tribe increase. In this pandemic and beyond it, may you find your dearest me.

– Bijayalaxmi,
New Delhi, August 2020

Introduction-2

You can't stay in your
corner of the forest
waiting for others to come
to you. You have to go to
them sometimes.

– *Winnie the Pooh*

Paul Romer, an American economist had once stated, "a crisis is a terrible thing to waste." *Thirty One Pandemic Letters* began to take shape during the peak of the COVID-19 crisis, when the human world was put in a lockdown mode by an invisible being without a form. It was during this immensely challenging period that an ancient friend of mine decided to lock herself down in a "silence mode"; I experienced lockdown within a lockdown and reached out to my childhood friend Bijayalaxmi via a WhatsApp text that I may have hurt a dear friend's feelings. Bijayalaxmi did not probe any further, yet she could glean my pain and she replied to my text through an email. Thus our journey began of exchanging letters with each other. Instead of falling apart in a crisis, we grew our branches of hope and positivity towards each other in the form of a chain of emails. During the course of our email exchanges, we decided why not we compile these letters into a book and share it with the rest of humanity.

The purpose of this book is to inspire readers to begin their journey of writing; through writing one has the immense potential to heal oneself. Even in the darkest periods of one's life, friendships can bring about a ray of light. Bijayalaxmi did just that by creating a "bridge over troubled water". Thirty-One Pandemic Letters is about our process of learning to be brave and strong and growing through daily humdrum of life. It is all about building bridges and not burning them. Our sincere hope is that this book will light up the flame within every reader to pick up a pen and paper and start writing, and spread the light of hope, and joy all around the world.

– Sangita Misra,
New York, August 2020

Illustrator's Note

Before joining the civil service, I had been a cartoonist and started getting published in the Indian Express when one day Arun Shourie, the editor of the Express, noticed one of my cartoons in his dak and published me for the first time under the Letter to the Editor (as suggested in my submission) and later-on on p.5. After having left drawing for almost three decades, the authors inspired me to pick up the pen again. This is my first foray into illustration.

Bijayalaxmi is a quintessential storyteller. She has an immense capacity to describe things vividly. This helped the artist in me to imagine. With Bijayalaxmi, I heard her describe to me what she wrote. With Sangita, I did not have this vantage point. I could draw inspirations only by reading her letters. I have tried to meet their expectations. Readers will judge me hereafter.

The cover illustration is based on Letter 3, where it appears again (p. 56). The illustration strives to capture the connection between the two childhood friends who came close over large distances with the pandemic looming large over the Earth. The mirror here is also a glass which you can see through. It also reveals how they view each other as reflections.

The illustration in the Introduction-1 (p. 35) depicts the pain and haplessness of reaching out to Ashee, our daughter, staying alone more than 10,000 km away in NYC. With no flights and no way to reach her, to see her, to hold her, this depicts the trauma on both ends.

The illustration in Letter 1 (p. 48) is of Cuttack's Barabati Fort, within the confines of which Bijayalaxmi lived in her childhood and where the 13 years something authors would often meet and sit there looking at the moat below. The second one (p. 51) shows Bijayalaxmi looking at the clear skies of Delhi during the Covid lockdown sipping tea in a contemplative mood.

The next illustration appears in Letter 6 on p. 66. It shows Sangita cooking in the kitchen with her son Sachin and the cat Mauli, who appear in her letters repeatedly.

The illustration in Letter 7 on p. 69 shows the authors sitting by the seaside in the Bay Area in Queens, NY looking beyond the horizon and sharing their memories, old and new!

Sangita, while writing Letter 10 on a rainy day, suddenly gets attracted to the conversation among birds who have started chirping after the rain stops. The illustration on p. 78, is a close study of a group of birds talking to each other.

In Letter 11, the illustration on p.80 depicts a multi-tasking Bijayalaxmi. During the lockdown period, she was cooking, she was cleaning, she was managing her college online, she was attending Zoom meetings and webinars, etc. etc. Simba, our pet, seems totally amazed seeing her cook, a rare sight otherwise!

The next one in Letter 14 on p. 91 shows the serene veranda of Sangita's childhood home in Cuttack. Her mother is selecting novels from the Kabuli Wallah from whose mighty sack magical books will emerge. A spellbound Sangita seems totally immersed!

I particularly love the illustration in Letter 15 on p. 95. Here Bijayalaxmi is talking about the memories that they have created together – in Cuttack, Puri, Sambalpur, Delhi, Kerala and New York. I happened to be with them in Kerala where we really enjoyed. The illustration depicts them in their bohemian self in the background of a Kerala temple.

I also love the illustration on p. 101 in Letter 17. Bijayalaxmi is talking about letters that Einstein wrote to his daughter invoking 'the power of love to replace every other power'. This prompted me to draw Einstein mocking the world on his iconic $E=mc^2$, while he kept his most powerful formula '$E=Lc^2$ (L= Love)' secret from the world, reserved just for his daughter.

In Letter 18 (p. 106), the illustration shows Bou (Bijayalaxmi's mother) sewing frocks for her three daughters sitting by the large window of the colonial bungalow in Cuttack. Sangita remembers her throwing large feasts for which she would have sewn dresses for the children. Bijayalaxmi has narrated this to me innumerable times!

In Letter 20, Sangita narrates how she came to know so much about Meera Bai through Bijayalaxmi's research. And she finds that her friend is a Meera in many ways. The illustration on p. 111 is a simple, elegant, immersed in dhyan Meera Bai.

In Letter 21 on p. 115 I have depicted a world hanging for its life on a giant N95 mask during the unprecedented Pandemic. In Letter 22 comes up my another favourite on p. 118. Sangita here is talking about how she relates to Ferdinand, the strongest and the largest bull in Spain. He is a bull who prefers to smell flowers rather than fight with other bulls. This imagery suddenly prompted me to remember the fierce Charging Bull of Wall Street, NYC. And I imagine the Fearless Girl, not standing far from the bull (earlier in front of it and now on nearby Broad Street), offering a bouquet of flowers to him. At once, there is a connection of love between them!

In Letter 24, Sangita is telling the story of Savitri and Satyavan to her inquisitive son Sachin. The illustration on p. 130 depicts the famous moment when Satyavan dies in a forest and the Lord Yama, God of Death, comes to take him to the other World.

In Letter 28, Bijayalaxmi is writing about the untimely demise of the authors' childhood friend Monali. The bird freed from the cage on p. 147 symbolises the soul leaving the worldly cage.

The last illustration in Letter 31 on p. 153 simply cheers the lovely friendship and strong bond between the authors.

Hope these illustrations do justice to this lovely collection of letters between two childhood friends.

– Rajesh Singh

21 December 2023

Glossary

Aloo Dum	:	Boiled potatoes in a gravy with spices
Bou	:	Mother
Dahi Bara	:	Deep fried lentil dumplings in yoghurt based sauce
Gajja	:	Saltine snack made from all purpose flour, ghee and cooking oil
Ghuguni	:	Boiled yellow peas or Black gram in a gravy served as accompaniment to several dishes.
Jagannath	:	Lord of the Universe
'Jagannatha kichi magu nahin tate .... shraddha baliru muthe'	:	Lord of the universe, all I am asking from you is a handful of sand filled with sincerity and faith.
Killa	:	Fort
Nana	:	Father
Papdi Chaat	:	Traditional fast food with saltine snack, boiled potatoes, coriander chutney, tamarind chutney, yoghurt.

Family Tree

BIJAYALAXMI'S SIDE

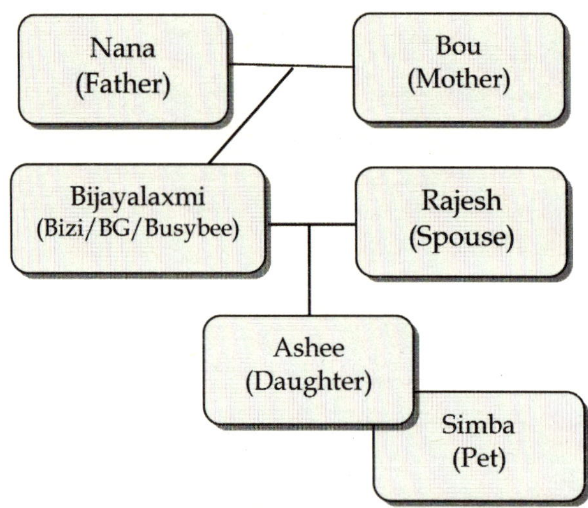

SANGITA'S SIDE

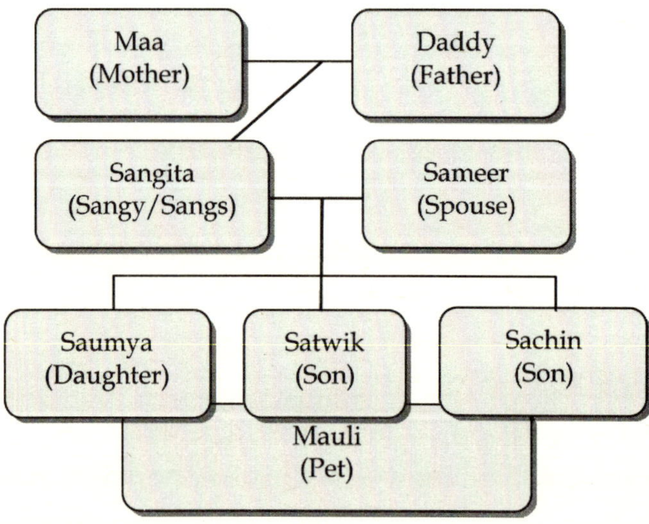

Letter 1

The Beginning: A Pandemic Reflection of our Forty Years of Friendship

– Bijayalaxmi, New Delhi,
26 April 2020

My dearest me,

Here we are at fifty-three years stuck in a dystopia that no writer could have ever imagined. I believe that Hollywood Films have and I tend to agree with the oft-quoted line "the fact is stranger than fiction". Yet is this fact that a virus supposedly from a wet market in Wuhan from a fluttering bat has made its way to our nightmares and locked us up in them?

Do you remember our first meeting? And all our old meeting places in our spring suffused adolescent days. The moat and the canals around us. Our favourite sitting place ... the jutting rock on the canal bed … the fort before us ... the river beyond that ... our imagination rested on the sailing moons and stars.

And then our stories of pain and joy intermingling with our laughter ringing bells in our hearts. If anywhere there was a charmed friendship it was ours. When we looked at each other we saw the mirror … a kinder mirror of a forgotten golden sunlight, torrential rains, and a spring waiting in the wings. Then we moved to different cities and fell in love with young men who wore their hearts on their sleeves and created images of themselves in our heads and we filled those who we imagined them to be. They fell short of our dreams. No heroes ... just young people

... human and flawed... like you and me and us.... I discovered the eyeliner and the fringe hair-cut with you. self-discovery of joyous beauty a mirror which held us with sparkling ready to overflow oceans....

And then again we were in different states in a physical and mental sense. A loss of a mother turning my world upside down no mirror can reflect the pain of separation from living and breathing loved ones... dead or alive. Your marriage coincided with my loss. And I guess we both came to terms with what we lost and what we gained.

And you chose a distant country and I chose a different alienness of a region within the country. My marriage mirrored yours too. And we let go of our dreams and resolutely followed our paths of life learning. I as a teacher and you a librarian and then a nurse. You with three children and me with one. Our daughters at 7 years exchanged dolls with each other. And we hoped one day they could discover this magical connection between themselves where distance or silence made no difference.

And my daughter at 18 years chose to travel to New York choosing your city to make it hers. And somehow it felt alright to me ... even if it was not how you and I wanted me to be in pain ... separation being our biggest nemesis.

And love ... loss longing and laughter we shared each story and laughed and cried over it. And we remain mirrors reflecting childhood stories in our eyes. Your mother and mine still live in them. Eternal as they are. Still as crystal-clear like the source of the Mahanadi river.

I visit your home in New York. Your warm nest of cats and birds and children and potential waifs you can bring in for your heart is so open. And you and your children on my bed in my Delhi home ensconced with the comfort of our reflecting love. One day soon I will come to you I say or you say and we believe each other for we know that our wings are real.

And this pandemic is a mirror too. Of our fears and our nightmares. That nothing is forever. Our wings are not for real. And we never know when we can be separated. A cold and fever have held us captive now and the words 'we will meet soon' seems the most implausible suddenly.

Here in Delhi I get up in the morning and clean and wash and cook a little. The laptop is my workplace now. I sit there working from morning to evening trying to make sense of the new contours of my workday. It seems unwieldy and soon it takes a shape of its own trapping me and making me a cog in its wheel. This wild juggernaut rolling around ... no human presence ... just this virtual world ... all touches now evil ... to be sanitized at every point. Nana and Rajesh float in this compact world and Ashee's absence the most real presence here.

I watch the sky from my balcony. The park is clean ... purple flowers have filled the branches of a tree across ... the sky is no longer polluted by the vehicles which have gone home to rest. It seems that Mother Earth has been given a break from every day churning of its internal entrails to fill our exotic materialistic desires....

But I feel the cavernous distance between us now ... especially that my daughter Ashee is there. I never felt it before. I knew I could reach you but now I know our hands will not touch each other nor can we hold each other ... for many, many days ... and no one knows when it will change....

I know of people who walked to their homes in far flung areas and died on their way ... poverty and pandemic giving them no choice... I know now my middle-class security will wait for wings for my legs are too fearful to walk so far....

I have not stepped out of my home for 4 weeks. Like a bird without wings ... like a proverbial bat I hang upside down on my second floor tiny apartment. Sometimes the Television and the internet like hallucinatory drugs take hold of me and sometimes I try to hold on to my imagination to give me flight.

Yet you are my mirror ... pandemic or not ... and one day I will find my feet and the skies will open and the Gods will heal the pain and protect our loved ones ... and we can return to our childhood rock and throw stones into the water ... and hold hands and hug each other....

What do you say my dearest me?

Love
Bizi

LETTER 2

A Lockdown within a Lockdown

– Sangita, New York,
27 April 2020

"You remember our first meeting?" Ah! You asked
So sweet it sounded
Like honey swirled around peanut butter Ah!
A slice of bread This life is Rye or White
Brown or sliced Ah!

A pair of lotus feet, hanging down from a weightless frame onto a green moat … all her weight lay in her palms, that held mine firmly; "we are in it together my dearest me" – silent words escaped from her palms onto mine – a warm feeling of belonging – ten tendrils intertwined – I felt I was safe around her, a place where I could bare my heart and naked soul and she would pick me up and clothe me with her dreams.

That those palms could pass on a virus so strong that it can kill, never passed our minds, as we gazed into the horizon and saw paper boats floating by. Did we ever wash our hands for 20 seconds, my dearest, after returning home? I do not recall ... all I remember is your hands clasping mine and giving me a world of strength that no virus can obliterate.

My dearest me, five decades of water has passed under our bridge, troubled waters. I sit here, 10,000 miles away, my aged fingers type slowly, giving form to my myriad of thoughts bursting through my brain. I want to thank you for continuing to trust me in this journey called life.

Even the best of friendships can crumble down with words that can be misconstrued.... I pray that we may never see this happen in this lifetime – for how can a reflection have a form without a form!

Just last night, I hurt a close friend's feelings so much that she has shut herself from me – she is in a lockdown mode during this time of lockdown. I wish I had locked down my fingers when they went about typing up words that formed grotesque shapes in my friend's brain beyond wildest imagination – I could have been clever, but I am not. My words may have hurt her feelings beyond repair, although they were meant to be a guiding light for the future. Instead, they fell like daggers into her heart and choked her into silence.

I wonder how would you have reacted to my words. I wonder, would you have closed the gates leading to your heart, by pointing out the cracks in me and then wished me peace?

I wonder about the fragility and frivolity of human bonds a simple word can shatter a mirror into millions of splinters....

And this pandemic is a mirror too. Of our fears and our nightmares. That nothing is forever. Our wings are not for real. And we never know when we can be separated.

Your words my dearest me ring true ... as if you read my mind ... and my thoughts....

A lockdown, within a lockdown...

Can a lockdown be a solution to any problem at hand? What do you say My Dearest Me?

Love and Light

Sangy

Letter 3

The Karmic Zoom

– Bijayalaxmi, New Delhi,
27 April 2020

My Dearest me,

Monday has stealthily crept up on me ... this lockdown making no difference to its twisted design to throw up its green bile of active guilt on me. I lay in bed feeling listless and sad ... words stuck in the pit of my stomach ... your email brings alive the magical world of our childhood ... Cuttack ... Killa Fort ... two words in translation meaning the same thing ... and yet stuck together ... no one questions why ... like mirror images ... yet different in phonetics ... now in a lockdown ... how do you think my beloved Killa Fort looks? The *Dahi-bara-alloo dum* that we ate every evening sold on the street in smelly buckets ... with water from the sea-green moat ... the old genial hawker's gnarled hands dipping into It ... I rarely washing my hands then ... holding onto yours ... eating street food ... throwing pebbles into the moat.

How could our hands become toxic like our minds slipping in and out? Only learning to fear and hate.... Our hands mimicking our minds....

Your friend will heal ... lockdowns between genuine friends may break with words too ... at least I think so ... my heart can never lock down somehow ... and I bless my mother for that ... she taught me by her early death ... that everything will soon end ... and no matter how hard we try we cannot reach out to each other with words ... for death is the permanent lockdown.

Delhi is my chosen home now, 1200 miles from our green moat ... your dancing eyes ... your silky tousled head and your unusual laughter like champagne glasses tinkling with each other, still ring over the moat of our childhood....

A sincere apology expressed with genuine words can open the lockdown between you and your friend ... I know it will....

I wonder how one apologizes to a pandemic? Washing hands singing happy birthday for I could never time myself on 20 seconds ... I forget many times why I am doing it. I look up at my mirror over the sink ... shadows of the night collected under my eyes....

A Zoom work meeting will need me to look cheerful and sincere and also provide hope to all who watch me expecting me to lead I can see my own face in the collected images of the Zoom meeting on my computer screen ... It is no mirror ... my own face ... it is a mask ... and I believe now I have to wear another one to step out into the open ... a mask over another to protect myself from a virus transmitted by human beings with such alacrity and virulence that multiple masks we wear to the world are not enough.

Monday it is ... let me find my way into this world of masks. No mirrors here ... no mirrors here.... I hope and pray the splintered mirror joins seamlessly and your friend smiles back at you.

I do not like to see you unhappy....
After all, you are my mirror....

10,000 miles away ... now getting ready for bed.... Saumya perched over her computer ... and Satwik too.... Sachin with his I-pad and Sameer watching TV and you putting your dishes into the dishwasher or maybe they are all around you helping you put them away ... and Sachin says, "A mirror is not a piece of glass with a reflecting surface eyes are also mirrors."

At least that is what I hear...

I will get on with my day as if it is normal the new normal is what they say ... and I laugh soundlessly nothing is normal and we pretend so ably ... this is life ... masks and lies ... this is the story of being adults....

But the lockdown will lift in phases they say ... and we have to get on and let Karma decide ... but is karma ever fair ... or does it wear a mask too?

So what do you say my dearest me?

Love!
Bizi

Letter 4

Masquerades

– Sangita, New York,
27 April 2020

It is 6:46 am and I have woken up since long. I am a morning person and the silence of the morning is when I am most productive as a mother ... the fish and the cat need to be fed. If I do not wake up in time, my cat will bite my ankle or Sachin will wake me up. "Mama, time for you to wake up, Maoli needs food". The fish ... their voices only I can hear ... "Ma" they say and wiggle their fins when they see me. They are locked down for 3 years now ... in a covered bowl of water that humans have given a fancy name. Many times, I have felt like releasing them into the ocean. "Flush them down the toilet, Mama, that will lead them straight into the ocean, they will gain freedom, but am pretty sure they will be eaten up in no time by the big fishes", says Sachin. "Fish", I corrected him. "Whatever," he says "There is a price to pay for freedom, death is the ultimate form".

How does one apologize to a pandemic? Your question Guess by singing "Happy birthday" and then giving ultimate freedom to a virus, by washing our hands off the matter ... a matter that something that occupies space and has weight now the matter at hand is occupying and throwing its weight about – the virus and the weight of a long-standing friendship that has become unfathomable. Both occupy space within and around me. I can wash the virus off with soap and water – How does one wash off a typed up text sent into space? One can't – they say "Whatever is sent into the internet, stays in the internet, it never leaves". It occupies ... a mere word ... and grows ... rather balloons ... a mere lockdown will not contain it. It needs a mindful lockdown, to delve into self-introspection and reflection – "Why did the word bite me like a poisonous snake?" It needs to clarify this very important question rationally and honestly Otherwise. it may blow out of proportion and create an atom bomb. A lockdown does not help the other party – building walls and fortresses around oneself does not help. The Great Wall of China could not contain the virus. A wall around the mind/heart will not as well - but there is no way to reach out – 'a sincere apology and genuine words' can only reach if a wall is penetrable. Guess, then – they say "Time is the greatest healer" – and aging may aid in quick healing....

"I do not like to see you unhappy....
After all you are my mirror...."

It comes out from my mouth reading your sentence in the form of a question "What is a mirror?" Sachin hears it....

"A mirror is but burnt sand."
"Is that so!" I exclaim.

"You didn't know that MAMA ... sand from the beach is put in a furnace and burnt to make glass...."

I look at him adoringly "I love you so much Sachin, but I don't know why."

"Me too, I have no idea, why you do?"

"I am your mother....maybe that is why."

"Whatever" – he grunts.

Soumya says – "I am tired of seeing your face all day," She says it matter of factly – no word mincing ... straight to the point.

"Take it as a blessing, one day I shall not be visible to you."

She quaffs – "Yeah right!"

She perhaps did not want to dive deep into my statement. And I being a mother, instantly forgave her for her unminced words ... 'Unminced' is not a valid word just like her statement. I did not take it into my heart. If I had, it would have led to unchartered territories and I did not want to traverse into such territories ... the world will throw barbs anyway ... we cannot be in a perpetual lockdown mode for that!

Our fortress My Dearest me – do you remember? It had a majestic gate – an open fortress; an oxymoron. The walls were invisible to the eye ... the ditches green – replete with algae. We were free to build walls within, but we learnt not to, from our mothers.

A mother's heart cannot build fortresses, it needs to remain open at all times; an open fortress, with a majestic gate to let karma in. Karma can be a bitch; karma can bite us in the ass – a mask will not fit mine. I remain unmasked.

A chilly wind blows outside, I tremble – my cup of tea is warm like your palms – let it soothe me and unmask my happiness within – after all, pleasantness and unpleasantness all is felt within us is a choice ... and you, My Dearest me. had said "Choice is a beautiful word".

I wonder what your world is throwing at you? Daggers? Knives?

Flowery nothings? Nothingness? Absolut Vodka? Peace?

Whatever it may be ... I am here to listen ... listen to your heart.

Let the masquerade begin – Cheers!

Hugs......

Love

Sangy

Letter 5

Sand Mirrors

– Bijayalaxmi, New Delhi,
28 April 2020

My Dearest Me,

How I wish I could mirror your lovely early morning sojourn of being needed.... Alas, I am no morning person much that I would like to be. My night stretches over an expanse of another day I think I stretch my night deliberately for my days are rented for work and do not seem to belong to me. Work emails and messages have scant respect for the night too... only I am not obliged to answer.

Ah, Sachin and his wondrous wisdom!

"A mirror is burnt sand". Perhaps we are burnt sand ... scorching heat of our life, loss and love has turned us so.

Reminds me of a *Jaganatha Janana*.

"Jaganatha ho kichi maggu nahin. tate .....maguchi Shraddha balli Ru muthe"....

(Lord of the universe, all I am asking from you is a handful of sand filled with sincerity and faith.)

I must find out the exact import of those lines and share with you. It is 10.12 am here. I have done my bed and got readied for sweeping the floor. In one hour I have to be ready to interface with my world of work. I am late today. Somehow, I get late everyday for work even if I am no longer travelling 23 km to my college. It is as if lateness is my curse ... a ghost possession of a different kind twisting me to be inadequate by being late.... A small sin you think? Maybe not. I must sleep early now and perhaps I will not be late....

The pandemic impacts our perception of time.... Suddenly we have lots of it or maybe we are running out of it.... It should make us resilient ... generous ... forgiving ... compassionate.... Yet it seems to twist us into grotesque shapes of anger, anxiety and anguish. Perhaps we all have a mirror that reflects our dark times. But like I said, "choice is a beautiful word".

I choose not to and I learn that from you ... my burnished golden reflecting sand of memories ... past ... present and future....

Saumya's words are like our mothers'. The unadulterated truth ... She knows no other. Actually, I say the same to Rajesh, "I am tired of seeing your face."

He smiles with absolute glee. He knows it is my way of expressing love. "Unminced words for those we love and trust the most".

My world is relatively silent at home. Phone calls to Ashee deliver even less noise. She whispers. "I am in a class ... I am eating ... I am on a call". Sometimes, she switches on her camera and takes me on a tour of her tiny white shell that she lives in ... beans ... rice and eggs ... sun from a streaming window ... a neat white desk with some of her heavy texts ... she seems happy ... this lockdown was what she was preparing for her whole life.... Quietly reading at the corner of my bed is how I saw her from the time she was 13 years old. Suddenly transforming from a garrulous little granny to a shadow of light silence....

I never understood why ... I have some explanations but not quite adequate like you said, "Mother's cannot build fortresses". They are just open doors and windows and perhaps true love should be like that ... but we put everything in compartments and give it labels ... and now the pandemic like a storm is laughing raucously at our labels.

Work from home ... work at home.... New normal....

So I get ready to masquerade as the good daughter, the good wife and the good principal ... suffering always from the imposter syndrome....

Tuesday is a bearable day they say I hope and pray the knots of pain unravel and you heal today. I know you are in bed ... your limbs spent and your heart heavy for you feel you could have avoided those words ... but those words were needed by this universe....

Let no nest lovingly built with care and caution be destroyed in this pandemic ... let us appreciate what we have than to yearn for what we do not. My prayers for Sameer who is serving the most noble cause of fighting to save lives without worrying for his own.

Brickbats and bouquets are all illusions ... all masquerades.... We have to evolve and learn that soon....

Time is of the essence as they say and the pandemic laughs ... "you never know!"

No vodka ... just apple juice from a tetrapack or freshly squeezed orange juice for breakfast.

My dearest me, a lockdown allows so much of our heart to open ... what do you say my dearest me?

Hugs
Bizi

LETTER 6

Pink Rage

– Sangita, New York,
28 April 2020

Morning has barked at me in the shape of a dog in a pink sweater; a bitch perhaps. She seemed mighty angry at her two walkers. She barked her way through her walk in front of my nest. The birds on the plum tree cheered her along with their chirping – a cacophony of multiple languages spoken together – who understood, deciphered what these voices wanted to convey? I interpreted the birds as a cheerful lot and the bitch in distress. But, hey, that is my interpretation - it could be the other way around....

Good Morning, My dearest me!
Good day to you
My fragile angel
With wispy wings
Let this day begin for me!

For you it is almost over ... with your bed made, and floors swept, and meetings attended on a virtual plane. Perhaps you took a break and sat next to Uncle and his soothing aura, and immersed yourself in Simba's unabashed affection ... or perhaps Rajesh smiled and hummed a tune....

The knots of pain, who can untie? Who ties the knots? Therein lies the answer my dearest me. Who can tie a knot inside us?

Sachin's burning question to me today was "Would you rather want to be a deer or a cow?" I was sprucing up a quick breakfast for him – a banana and peanut butter sandwich. He asked for tea and waited for my answer.

"A cow in India, perhaps, so I can be revered." or simply a cow in the green countryside ... but then why not a deer?? Yes, that will do too By then, he had left "blowing his funny away". That is a term he uses when he cannot control his smile and uses his small palms to brush off the smile from his lips. "Blowing the funny away".

Sameer came down in his pink bathrobe and pink slippers – his hair long and grey and shaggy – In the lockdown phase, the locks have grown. I look at him – so very at ease in that colour meant for girls, in this country – Pink and Blue have a gender – "Real men wear pink" is also a slogan here to dare a man to wear that shade.

My friend Sujita asks "How are you S?"

My response – S straddles, stumbles, stutters, shakes, shivers, sleeps, sings, suffers, sighs, sexy siren, strong, silently sways, softly – the shape of S is the curviest amongst all alphabet – no jagged edges, or straight, sharp line S.

My friend's response – Sameer, Sangita, Satwik, Sachin, Saumya

It is interesting how different people invoke/evoke different ways to express ourselves. With you, it always has been poetry, silence and prose. We can pen down our thoughts for hours or simply sit in serene silence together holding hands and gazing into nothingness.

Ashee, "in her shadow of light silence" – how beautiful, and yet how tough on a mother to be staying far away. A brave soldier you are! I have learnt that from you – how to stand strong in the face of a storm and carry on. You had said you have two pillars in the shape of a father and husband. They are pillars, true, and yet and yet.

We all are here on borrowed time, My dearest me even Corona. One day she will cease to live and so also us. She has one life to live and so also us. She wants to live desperately, so also us. She clings to us to breathe life into her and we have to stop breathing for her so she can live, still she dies and when we die, because she cannot live inside a dead body. We cannot either....

Have you pondered over this matter, My dearest me?

Love and blessings and thanks for keeping the channels of communication open – openness begets openness, love begets love ... let us choose well. Like Goethe said, "Choose well, your choice is brief and yet endless". The words I chose were meant well, and yet the silence is endless. Does silence beget silence?

What do you say my friend!

Love and Kisses
Sangita

Letter 7

Common Cold Gone Rogue

– Bijayalaxmi, New Delhi,
29 April 2020

Your morning description makes me giggle … it uplifts my spirits. I have not stepped out at all in a whole month. And I feel the bittersweet cold of your happy New York minted pink froth of a morning.… I feel inspired ... maybe, I should go for a walk too ... maybe in the evening so I can describe the Delhi exterior world to you.… Except that Delhi outdoors look promising but their streets are treacherous … uneven sly ones.... I hate to walk here. New York is a place to walk … really … it is walkable. I remember my walks with you in the park near your home or the one at the Bayside.… Both times we recreated our childhood scene in Cuttack. Always Cuttack at Queen's New York … never in Delhi … She is not amenable to adapt to that at all.... I want to walk though just for you spread my arms a little… osteoporosis is locking them down … and hours on the phone and computer too… hunkered down .... interesting American expression….

I love your description about the letter S and your delightful conversation with both Satwik and Sachin. So inspired and full of spontaneity are your words. I bless them both for bringing you joie de vivre and restoring your mojo ... your beautiful essence....

While your breakfast for Sachin as well as his question both intrigue me I must tell you I prepared an authentic Odia dinner yesterday at the same time … rice, Dalma, Tomato Khatta (Chutney) and Allu Chakta (mashed potatoes). I am amazed when I serve the food on the plate … as if they appeared by magic … having outsourced all our domestic work to our wonderful part-time helps … the pandemic has made me discover my self-sufficiency … although I am nowhere near their efficiency.

Yes, I feel brave but I am brave too because you are there as if a part of me is there in New York looking out for her … a sweet silvery scintillating shower silently shyly swaying over her … a song of songs … my dearest me….

A virtual meet awaits me … I am one minute late … Sachin's question yet to be answered by me ... but I am blowing my funny away is such an evocative line ... it cheers me as does your nonchalant Sameer in pink….

The pandemic needs to make peace by not killing, that is its aim I think … then we can exist peacefully … herd immunity ... is all the pandemic wants to achieve … praying for that.... I think this way we all can live in harmony … just a common cold gone rogue….

Off to my paranoid paradoxical workplace of intense connectivity in times of physical distancing….

Your quote from Goethe reverberates with me…

Let us choose well…

And then our favourite quote from Gone with the Wind mouthed by Scarlett O'Hara, "Tomorrow is another day!"

My hopes for all of us including Scarlett is that.

I am already in the tomorrow of your today … how surreal are time zones.

My dearest S .... sleep well…

From your
Busybee

LETTER 8

Living in Harmony

– Sangita, New York,
29 April 2020

The silence of the morning was awoken by three sneezes from Sachin. "God Bless You", I said three times. What a blessed way to begin this Wednesday! A beginning with blessings to a little soul who asked "Mama, do you have a college fund for me? How much money is in it so far?"

"20K maybe ... not sure".

"Will that be anything?"

"Just to wade you through".

"Will I have to take up a minimal pay hourly job then to pay off my college debts in 5 years?"

"I am not sure, depending on what college you choose."

"By then, we will have a housing crisis, America is going downhill, there are corrupt politicians, maybe 0.0001 % care about us, if at all."

"And the ones we think they care about, I wonder as well. "

The tea kettle screamed and broke my line of thought – Sachin left with his bread and nutella with a cup of milk in his hands. The online school will start soon.

Your dinner preparation brings back nostalgic memories of my stay at your place. You took pains to serve Sachin dahi bhata (curd rice) on your bed – placing a lap desk for him so that he gets comfortable. Simba sat next to him, looking eagerly for a bite or two, his tail lightly wagging and tongue out. Your finely made bed was messed up by us – you did not frown, rather on your face was a serene look of satisfaction. I will never forget that moment. Thank you for giving that gift to us. You also wore pink! But there was nothing bitchy about that – a serene pink that made you look more becoming – now that I come to think of it, pink is your color – there are so many shades of it, yours is a Benjamin Moore's "Pink Hibiscus" – subtle, soft, soothing and sensitive. But then you always look like a Goddess in a bold mustard yellow! I guess that is the side of your Durga Avatar. The Avatar you take upon as a leader of a massive institution for women.

Your description of the pandemic – "A common cold gone rogue", made me reflect upon the hurt that I caused to an ancient friend of 44 years. Two common words put together created an atom bomb. Was it my making?

"You have no tact" Soumya says that to me often. "That is how Sagittarians are, they mean well, but they are blunt".

It does pain me to inflict pain upon someone. The birds chirp outside in unison as I type up my thoughts – they are sitting on the branches of the Plum tree. The branch of the Plum tree has reached out to me, towards my nest almost onto the French window. I expressed to Sameer – "There are bird droppings daily on our patio."

"How can it be solved?"

"It can be solved if I call the management, if I call them, they will cut the branch. If the branch is cut, the birds will lose their meeting space and cutting off the branch will hurt the tree."

Sameer said "Then, you will have to live with the poop, that is all!"

He said it in a matter of fact way, making no din. I like that about him – he is very accommodating to other living species. He could have said "The birds can find another branch to sit upon" or "Sangita, the tree branch is encroaching upon our property, let me call the management and get rid of this nuisance now".

Cutting off a branch is not a solution to any problem at hand ... that is how I feel. What are your thoughts on this, My Dearest me? The busy bee must know as well coz the bee has faced the biggest storm in her childhood and lived elegantly thereafter. Shakha (branch) – proshakha (bough?) ... both so very essential to survive ... cutting off a limb is so hard for some, yet so easy for others.

Like my once upon a time friend, Denise said, "Your dad losing your mom, is as if he lost one of his limbs".

In this journey of life, we meet, we mate, we sow our seeds, and then we depart.

I am blessed to be having this forum to voice out my thoughts to you. I hope my apology to my friend, reaches her and reaches in a healing way rather than again being misconstrued. But silence says a lot. How can one interpret silence? Muting notifications is an answer to many, to stop the cacophony of words reaching their ears, but it has never been my cup of tea ... if a branch reaches out to me. I let it sway softly serenely silently.

Love and hugs!
Sangita

LETTER 9

Red Coat in Times Square

– Bijayalaxmi, New Delhi,
30 April 2020

I thought I would write to you every morning ... choosing all my kaleidoscopic songs for you my dearest music of my heart.

But work seized me like a pandemic fear and churned me to a robotic shape staring into a computer screen ... work meetings ... a webinar on how gender violence has increased in the time of the lockdown and finally another work meeting for some submission deadlines...

Your description of that day about Sachin settled on my bed eating dahi bhata (curd rice) ... Simba wagging his tail ....

It was a moment of immense joy ... he is your spitting image and holds an ancient wisdom.... I feel complete when I am with you ... Your generous dining table filled with scrumptious dishes and the blackboard announcing our arrival. I feel so much a part of you, as if I do not know where you end and where I begin ... a seamlessness....

And Red is your colour ... Red coat warmth and your lazy walk down the Times Square ... no pretensions ... no airs ... a healing joyous smile ... you are the red warmth of kitchen and fireplace fires....

Red also of the Goddess who resides in us ... Durga ... our dearest me....

Sameer has many lovely qualities ... his ability to let you be ... yes let branches be ... let them reach out and touch us from the skies ... bring the skies to our homes....

I hope your olive branch will be accepted by your warring friend. I have let my branches grow extending to all but my roots firmly planted....

Any time someone can prune and cut and reject a branch but we have to hold on to mother earth firmly my dearest me ... we have to hold on ... and when we cannot we can turn into a bird and take the flight to the open skies....

Today is a sad day ... two memorable actors Irfan Khan and Rishi Kapoor die one by one succumbing to cancer ... both dealt well with their impending death ... with dignity and grace ... their spouses were their main support.

It makes me think that we need to take care of our health and our spouses too. I read out our letters to Rajesh ... he says. "It is a book already" I tell him now, "I was not able to write a letter today in the morning"... He shrugs nonchalantly, "Write one tomorrow in the morning".... and goes off to sleep. I switch on the television and skip through Netflix.... I get back to writing this email ... we are on the same day.... the earth circling the sun.

And it is already midnight here....

But it is still a letter for Thursday ... a letter for every day ... branching out to each other....

My dearest me! We are just letters branching out to each other....

Sending you love,

Bizi

LETTER 10

Of Chirping Birds and the Past

– Sangita, New York,
30 April 2020

My dearest me!

I could gauge you must have turned into a robot in order to manage mundane activities of living. It is a great ability we have as humans to switch back and forth from automatons into humans and vice versa. It is when we turn into rocks that changes the whole spectrum of living. A rock can give support or become a sitting place for the weary traveler but cannot let the ocean flow into it ... you have been a rock to me though and, strange as it may seem, you have melted into a river and immersed yourself in me "seamlessly". You have been a rock and a river to me but there are times rivers go into the ground and dry themselves out ... if at all let it hit the parched earth and turn into vapour, then into clouds and then rain all over again! Petrichor! It did exactly that after decades. We lost each other on the physical plane but fate brought us back together after my mother passed on to the alternate universe.

APRIL 30, 2020 8:30 am

Here the rain is slashing hard.... Morning time, I inadvertently decimated a swarm of ants in our cat Maoli's food plate – they got drowned while washing her bowl. I remembered Maa used to keep "Jala Jantra" (a local instrument using water to keep away ants) to keep ants at bay – I prepared one – took a plate, put some water and then placed her food bowl that was surrounded by an oasis of water, so no ants can traverse, as they have not learnt to swim yet. Hopefully, that will work and ants will not get killed unnecessarily. But they reside inside plant pots – the plants need to be watered. Why do they choose such silly places to build their homes? Why don't they learn from their past mistakes? Is it too alluring to give up space – that they would rather die than let go of a dangerous habit of residing in places where they surely will drown. Aren't many of us like the ants in my nest? We tend to become KALIDASA we cut the same branch that we sit upon....

Today Sachin is silent after asking me the morning question – "Mama would you rather shoot a snake or eat a donkey alive?"

He always puts me in a spot, asking such difficult questions. He says he tests my psyche, so he can know what his mother is all about.

Sameer sits here silently sipping tea and expressing sadness for Irfan Khan and Rishi Kapoor. I mull over my actions of drowning the ants – what kind of karma I built? Who to save, how ? All these questions fire in my brain and I look out the window for an answer – the wind is blowing gently and the wind chime chimes a sweet melody. Today no birds on the branches – the rain has driven them away someplace safe. I wonder if rain feels the way I do – how to rain so it does not have to kill anything and yet keep the earth nourished? Does it have a free will to choose where to rain? All these senseless thoughts arise in my head.

Satwick had commented on what is there to write daily to a friend when all I am doing is sitting most of the time on a kitchen chair?

"Mama what can you write day in day out? It is running over the same old ground."

The rain has finally stopped – I can hear the chirping of the birds.... let me listen to them and try to figure out what they are chattering about?

Love and hugs!
Sangy

LETTER 11

Between a Rock and a Hard Place

– Bijayalaxmi, New Delhi,
1 May 2020

Between a rock and a hard place today....

Here I am your loyal rock and flowing river lying on my bed ... writing to you 10,000 miles away from you ... lying in bed ... evening here ... morning there....

A warm sultry summer in Delhi ... the summer of May 2020. Each night Delhi promises a lot of things ... spring fresh grass and flushed red cheeks but by day it is like an ageing street-walker ... peddling her body for tea and five hundred rupees ... she knows who she is and does not care anymore....

Maybe it is nice to know who we are or may be not?

I cooked some ghuguni and cabbage curry ... Rajesh serves me breakfast everyday ... toasted bread, a boiled egg and watermelon juice ... we exchange a few rushed words and my workday begins. I cook lunch too and keep to my work desk ... webinars ... work meetings and emails ... then sharing my virtual workday with Nana even if he is actually just there right next to me ... it seems I have entered a sci-fi novel....

Simba was most puzzled to see me sweeping the floor his quizzical expression is definitely one to be amused about....

Sachin's questions may have deeper meanings … a cow or a deer ... save a snake or the zebra….

"We got carried away all right, its time we came to our senses. We are all in a mirage.... We amount to no more than mirages...," Dostoevsky's *Idiot* ends with these lines ... maybe not the exact lines but something like this.... Lizaveta Prokofyevna says this in a burst of anger for being stuck in a foreign land and not being able to go back to where she belongs ... it is about us I feel – you and me.

I forget stories now but I love to read the last lines of novels ... a finality ... about how life may turn out ... as if answers lie in a writer's imagination even if it is a Dostoevsky writing in a different time in an alien land....

Satwik is right ... every day what do we write? But I do take time to weave something for you and make myself return to my essence and make you my muse ... and every day seems less burdensome now ... so much to say ... and so much to hear things no one else has time or desire for? The words that really matter no one has any time for it ... they only want to speak of every day in terms of routines and surviving and somehow the magic of the everyday disappears in the curve of the road ... the tail end of a rushing car....

The lockdown has been extended till 18 May 2020 in India. What and how do we decide between lives and Livelihoods? Many will suffer and some will die of the disease and many will die of grinding poverty what hope can we give them?

Hallucinatory smoke rings around me....
My answer for Sachin:

Between deer and cows

Whys and hows

Zebras and donkeys
Snakes and monkeys

The charmer and the charmed

Who harms and who is harmed?

Who shall we be?

"To be or not to be?"

We could be butterflies in a digitally vibrant garden ... our wings brightened by a Snapchat app....

I am sending my fluttering finger butterflies to you and with a magical touch in this email, it will fly to you this very minute....

Imagine ... imagine....

My multi-coloured rainbow!

Love
BG

LETTER 12

Reading Dostoevsky in Corona Times

– Sangita, New York,
1 May 2020

Today has been a blase morning. The kind of morning that one may have nothing to talk about. From Satwick's perspective – "same old, same old". Sachin is even quiet as a mouse – a question was put forth but was cut short by his father. "Stop asking meaningless questions".

"But they have a lot of meaning Papa", – he interjected. I asked, "What was your question?"

He said, "Too late now, the time is gone". He was silenced for the time being. I hope not forever, because I enjoy his questions even though I have no answer to them that would sound acceptable. Still, as per him, he can gauge a lot from my answers.

In your part of the world, the lockdown has been extended to two more weeks. Over here in NY, there never was a strict lockdown to begin with. People still take walks and take their dogs for a run. Children still cycle, skate and run around.

I am typing up this letter to you in the background: the pitter- patter of raindrops, birds singing, plum tree branches swaying. Yesterday the plum tree was literally shaken up by fierce winds, creating a gaping hole around it. The possibility of it cracking under pressure was high. But it remained rooted. The branches helped to let it remain rooted – they swayed in harmony with the wind, so that the trunk does not lose its ground. The branches took the pressure from the trunk....

I think about the poor and the homeless – in this time of the pandemic, the plight of the daily laborers – the homeless people of NY, sleeping inside subway trains, defecating and urinating. The conductors are terrified of catching other kinds of viruses besides Corona.

A bright yellow tulip stares at me from its vase. It was lying listless outside on the paved ground. I saw it from the window and went and fetched it. I could give it a home because it is a tulip – what if it was a homeless person? Could I have lifted him from the ground and brought him in? I stare at the tulip with rapt attention.

My reverie was broken by Sachin – "Mama, I am dead".

Your interpretation of Sachin's questions – I am musing upon them. How the human brain interprets words ... his father found them nonsensical and you find deep meanings! I am stuck "between a rock and a hard place" like you ... because I have to answer fast and within a certain time frame, otherwise it becomes too late and the question becomes redundant....

Lizaveta, us and the Corona – we all are stuck in the foreign host as short term guests. May all of us heal, instead of being killed by our own illusions and delusions.

Signing off
Sangy

Letter 13

Dying in the Arms of Trees

– Bijayalaxmi, New Delhi,
2 May 2020

Much beyond a Saturday

An apathetic morning ... you say ... some uncomfortable silences ... and some questions and some answers... Sameer is practical ... his hands knowing life from death ... the vulnerability of the physical form ... he has no time for the innate philosophy of Sachin's questions ... it is understandable....

And Sachin always amazes me with his astute answers ... unless he is annoyed by something he will definitely answer your question no matter how unrelated it is to his sphere of things...

Your plum tree mirroring your generous spirit ... may it stand tall and may its branches allow each bird to rest awhile on it...

I have no idea if people are moving around in the city here. I have not stepped out for 35 days. It does not bother me at all ... and this thought bothers me a lot. Is it because my spirit is so full and so encompassing and I am so self-realised with no wandering needs or I am just so depressed that it does not matter now to me that I am just rotting away in a two and a half bedroom second floor flat!

I remember reading in a book somewhere these intriguing lines: "My grandmother died in the blue arms of a jacaranda tree. She could read thunders".

In my life I have died in the blue ... green ... yellow ... purple hued arms of many a tree and yet I cannot read thunder ... so is Sachin talking about that kind of dying...?

My heart feels a personal anguish for all those migrant workers walking to their homes ... hunger tearing and searing into their lungs ... their hunger had brought them to the cities and their hunger has driven them back...

I have never known real hunger ... how can I understand their anguish ... but I feel their pain rising and ebbing like the sea of Puri in Odisha captured in my childhood memory. The homeless are citizens of one country ... it is called hunger ... the homeless defecating and urinating on the roads of New York or the interiors of Odisha... Hunger is one country...

You know I am not fond of old photographs. It reminds me of too much of all that is lost ... but the citizens of the country of hunger make me realise this abstract feeling of loss is my sheer indulgence ... the privileged sorrow of the food-filled stomach...

... I wonder why I cannot share snippets of conversation of my day with you ... but I must admit that the conversations around me are monosyllabic. Nana and Rajesh are both gentle presences and I value them like one does the life-giving sunlight ... yet and yet ... I long for a soul conversation...

So I am blessed to have this form of speaking out to you ... my mirror of stars and secrets...

I sometimes think of how Jane Austen and the Bronte sisters spun their stories when women were only meant to reproduce and knit.

What mad courage drove them? I also think of the discipline of writing ... as an academician and some forays into creative writing I know discipline is far more than all the magical inspiration and genius you innately are borne with ... look at the discipline of the virus ... it mutates and breaks and spreads and kills true to its nature ... but if developed nation-states had been disciplined in spending a little more on health care and preventive protocols for mutating viruses then maybe this lockdown would not have taken place. It is not a war but a public health crisis and we don't need corona warriors but healers.

This primitive language of war is indeed maddening. The discipline of peace ... can it be inculcated?

Micheal Ondaatje, the beautiful, beautiful half Sri Lankan writer, quotes Jane Austen from her lesser known novel *Persuasion* in his chronicle about his family and it surprises me...

A man reading a woman quoting her words to describe his feelings ... why cannot world leaders speak of peace and kindness and empathy ... they are human beings. Are they not?

Or are they mutated varieties? The virus for whom we have no vaccine...

Is this truly only a disease ... a public health issue ... or a searing madness of egocentric capitalists in nexus with predatory political heads...?

Like you said, let us clear our heads of all our illusions and delusions ... and then what do we have...

Was it that Pink Floyd number...

I cannot remember it well.

Something that Satwik said,

"...what have we found.... The same old ground..."

Or someone else said it!

I cannot remember ... but I know you do remember and you will tell me ... you know what that means ... it means that your memory is mine too ... and my forgetting is not really so....

Ashee's friend told me, "It was our time to think of possibilities ... and now we are only thinking of the impossibilities."

Impossible times for the young...

My prayers for them...

Love to you ... my memory bank of Pink Floyd lyrics and childhood petunias...

Yours,

Busybee

Letter 14

Kabuliwallah and Summer Stories

– Sangita, New York,
2 May 2020

My Dearest myself,

What a surreal letter you wrote! It weaved yesterday and tomorrow and amalgamated it into the now. "The now" being our present meditative state of profound awakening. You sitting inside your cave for 35 days in deep contemplation. Is this called "Nirvana" or stagnation? It might be for many sinking into a mighty depressive state. But you and I have resorted to writing.

Something my mother had always encouraged me to do so – "Sangita, start writing, daily – keep a diary and write, whatever comes to your mind – write – keep at it – do not stop until you stop. Santanu Acharya set a time to write daily. He had a pen and paper in his hand and sat down. That is how he was able to write so many stories". She always quoted Santanu Acharya, when it came to me developing the art of creative writing. She had seen him in action, whenever she visited their house. Perhaps that scene stuck in her mind. My childhood thoughts were thus shaped by the writings by the novelist. His experimentations with magical realism inspired me especially his short story *Plus Minus Greater than Zero.*

The pandemic has brought about the creative side in many people. Sameer is indulging in a lot of gourmet cooking. He follows a man's blog called "Spice eats" and experiments with spices, yoghurt and heavy cream. Our nest has a perpetual aroma of freshly cooked greens and cheese drowning in an array of bright colored gravy. Soumya, on the other hand, is dabbling with growing radishes, scallions, Greek basil and leeks from seeds. She uses biodegradable egg cartons and organic dirt, to grow them into tiny seedlings. She fusses over them like a harried mother, scurrying around and tweaking their tiny limbs, quenching their thirst with droplets of water and sunning her little babies for a blast of chlorophyll. These seedlings have a home, a mother to fall back on...

Ah, there are so many forms of death... Sachin alluded to "procrastination" – online school and the immense possibilities of procrastination and not completing assignments on time. "Mama, I am dead", resonates the frustration of having unlimited time at hand, which leads to forgetfulness. And your quote, from a writer "my grandmother died in the blue arms of a jacaranda tree. She could read thunders"... takes me back to Burla days, where I used to rest on the branches of a Guava tree, and immerse myself in Jane Austen and Bronte sister novels. These novels were purchased by Ma, from Kabuli Wallahs, who carried these precious jewels inside sun tanned knapsacks. Ma used to invite them to our sprawling open verandah. The old, bent man would open the mighty sack and spread the books in front of us – my eyes would glint like precious stones, as I picked the novels with quivering fingers.

Old photographs and old memories mirror each other ... they bring us down on our knees.

Rajesh, silently prepping up boiled eggs and toasts for you, so you could begin your gruelling day of virtual meetings and separation – indeed it is a silence

pregnant with words! And uncle ... he speaks through his divine aura – one can get enlightened in his presence – Rumi comes to mind. "Silence is the language of God, all else poor translation". Our dear fathers who have enriched our lives by their silent presence. They are the oxygen we have breathed all our lives.

A man can only court a woman through quoting her line of thoughts and dreams ... a successful male writer knows how to market his memoirs ... on the other hand, a successful woman writer quotes her own life experiences – she weaves wings in her sentences and gives her breath to let it soar...

Let you and me soar invisibly through space, like Corona, and make our presence felt silently...

No more "running over the same old ground" and finding "same old fears", no more "two lost souls, swimming in a fishbowl, year after year". Yes, My Dearest Me, a Pink Floyd song , where one friend wrote for another friend, who had lost his mental faculties to LSD.

Yes, I wish you were here ... how I wish you were here.... I really do...

Sangy

LETTER 15

Memories of Incandescent Ice

– Bijayalaxmi, New Delhi,
3-4 May 2020

May 3 and 4, 2020 time 11.24 pm

Your beautiful nest full of the aroma of freshly cooked food wafts into my home ... a contrast to mine in many ways ... my cooking brings insipid dishes to the table which Nana loves....

There is a purity to insipidity he says ... there is nothing tempting about it.... I love it too somehow.... It is a denial of the baser instincts I feel ... a kind of righteous food ... so it is calming because we expect nothing of it. Sameer's chef avatar is indeed an eye-opener. I am intrigued by this transformation and bless it from a far....

And I close my eyes to find all of you in your dining room ... the mirror giving it a depth of the expanse of the blue ocean ... and all your knick-knacks come alive like a Van Gogh painting of flowers. The deepest blue on a peacock feather ... colours drawn only from a vivid imagination....

Saumya's fledging garden ... a unique experience ... of plants growing out of eggs ... and chickens growing on trees...

A discovery of a world of opposites .... Lewis Carroll would have been very happy with her ... she is indeed a serious Alice in a wonderland of her choice....

We are Silly Alices of blunder lands of our choices....

The significance of choices ... either they create wonders or blunders and you have to make your peace with it ... your quote from Goethe mentioned in your first letter indeed sums it up well.

I am not able to sleep anymore. It's my unfinished tasks that claim me as lovers possessively and completely and like I did with lovers of my past ... these tasks I resist....

Completely and vociferously...

The uncertainty of Ashee's life also makes me feel I am a woman with no feet.... Just stumps of unclassified human flesh. Then, there is the certainty of Mitu's death which comes to haunt me every night. Unfortunate only a connection by blood makes grieving a right through ritualistic practices. I want to cry about the unfairness of her death ... twin daughters a brave woman who fought relentlessly for them rejected by her spouse. Beloved of her parents and the apple of my eye.... I cannot cry ... like a woman with no eyelids....

No feet ... nor eyelids ... like a glorious mutated version of me ... clothed in my anguish.

She filled my life with a robust joy of a different kind something I was not used to.... "Ma' am the kids want to see you"... and there she would arrive like a friendly thundering storm enveloping my home and sometimes my entire existence. There are so many things that have been left unsaid by us.... How are we going to make amends now? Death, so firm and so resolute.

For three months, one summer three years back, we started writing Mitu's story.... Together on my little dining table. Typing away on my laptop her story is incomplete in its writing of it of course, and then now her life is over.... Done ... and it cannot be revisited and even if I did revisit it would not be the same.

Not without her ... never without her ... my brain screeches with an unresolved pain...

......

Alien fingers digging into my precious protected nine-year skin in a hot sweltering evening under a mosquito net ... I feel the blood of my tongue bitten by my teeth in my mouth....

Memories are incandescent frozen ice ... they reflect the light of the sun and the floating moon ... they bring back the thorns of the cactus too ... impinging on your thoughts ... like thumbnails on a college notice board.

Memories are like chocolate wrappers in between pages of an old diary....

Memories like winter rains....

Now everything is a memory in seconds ... instant photos make it so ... and you become nostalgic about a memory that happened two minutes back....

Memories of you and me in Cuttack, Puri, Sambalpur, Delhi, Kerala and New York.... I am so glad ... so joyous I have these memories of us....

Cream cotton sarees in gold borders and go-go glasses....

You and me laughing aloud at the list of 7 surprises lined up by our handsome young guide Arun Nayar. Rajesh half amused and half angry at our adolescent giggles...

We never let a chance pass by us to live in the moment....

We are....

And no pandemic will take away that...

We will be...

And no pandemic can change that too...

My dearest S... this is the end of my Monday and the beginning of my Tuesday....

And I owe you one more letter for a Sunday... Soon my dearest soon,

Bizi

Letter 16

Samba Dance and Herbal Cures

– Sangita, New York,
4 May 2020

"Perhaps the earth can teach us

As when everything seems dead in winter And later proves to be alive.

Now I'll count up to twelve

And you keep quiet and I will go."

The Chilean poet's words flow and Bebel croon's a Samba "Deixa", whilst I lay listlessly on my bed typing up this letter to you – "Deixa", translates into English as "leave" ... leave before the mask falls off "Meu amor"; I am your "Pierrot" in this old samba dance – I am your mask in this crazy dance called life. Life is a pantomime ... your friend played a part creating an illusion of reality. You got sucked into her act – the scene is over, the curtain drawn – she left the scene, and you carry on with her memories – an unfinished life, an unfinished tale in your eyes – the veil needs to be lifted off.

My dearest friend, this story of our lives has no end – like Scheherazade and her tales. You and I are doing just that – one letter a day to keep our head fixed in its place.

Ashee, Soumya and this generation, and Corona. It is a war between one virion and the rest of humanity ... in a world of possibilities, resides a world of hope. One thing I know for a fact, nothing lasts forever; change is inevitable. A new wind will blow for our children – "tomorrow will be another day". The wind that went is gone, and gone with it, the past. The memories are the dust – but a dust in the wind. We all are specks of dust in the wind – some of us invisible.

The food at your place has a blandness about it, which is soothing to the stomach; white noise. I slept for one whole day, after eating in your nest – a deep, restful sleep, in your bedroom. You had left for work leaving me to my dreams. Simba slept by my side on the floor, both breathing in harmony. You made the room dark, drawing the curtains and switching off the light and said to me – sleep. I did. Thank you for that.

Monday has slipped by for you – it still exists for me – "I have promises to keep ... and miles to go before I sleep". Today my throat is hurting, a dry cough and a headache. Corona echoes through the dark and deep woods of my mind. Perhaps she is a myth when it comes to my body – a fictitious character that simply exists in my head. In reality, my aches and pain stem from a different source that has no name....

My friend Vicki writes: "The princess wends her way through the green passage, treads lightly on a carpet of pink petals and arrives at the grove of the bleeding hearts". Your heart feels heavy and is bleeding ... let me chant a prayer for you to heal.

You do not owe me anything, My Dearest me ....

"Let go of this unpleasant way of being,

Roll my love,

Dance please,

Samba like that,

Sing for me,

whisper like that,

Come with everything love"

...Bebel Giberto croons in Portuguese ... music is a universal language of pain....

Let me heal you and through you, I heal as well. Love

Sangy

Letter 17

Dalai Lama and Fred Rogers

– Bijayalaxmi, New Delhi,
5 May 2020

The healing song...

I am worried about your dry cough

The fears from Corona are not old.

A dry cough runs a shiver down my spine ... something which earlier would mean having a cup of warm tea or gargling....

But I let your Samba dance and sing uplift me to a transcendental stage...

We can heal with love....

I believe Einstein wrote letters to his daughter that he said should not be published because their time had not come. The letter talks about the powerful force of love as transcending every other force. He invokes the power of love to replace every other power. Love can heal. It is the only force that defies logic. The time of love has arrived. So I heal you sending you my love ... the art of reiki healing. I have faith that my love for you is far more powerful than a mutated virus ... playing hide and seek...

With the human kind...

It has been a strange day.... I am contemplating on my own growth...my anxieties and fears.... I watched this beautiful movie called *A Day in the*

Neighborhood. Perhaps. Tom Hanks plays a beloved TV Host Fred Rogers. The character is who I want to be like a Dalai Lama ... content in your own skin yet giving importance to each person as if their lives are the most important stories we have witnessed. But is it easier for those who have achieved a certain status to be like that? So secure in themselves....

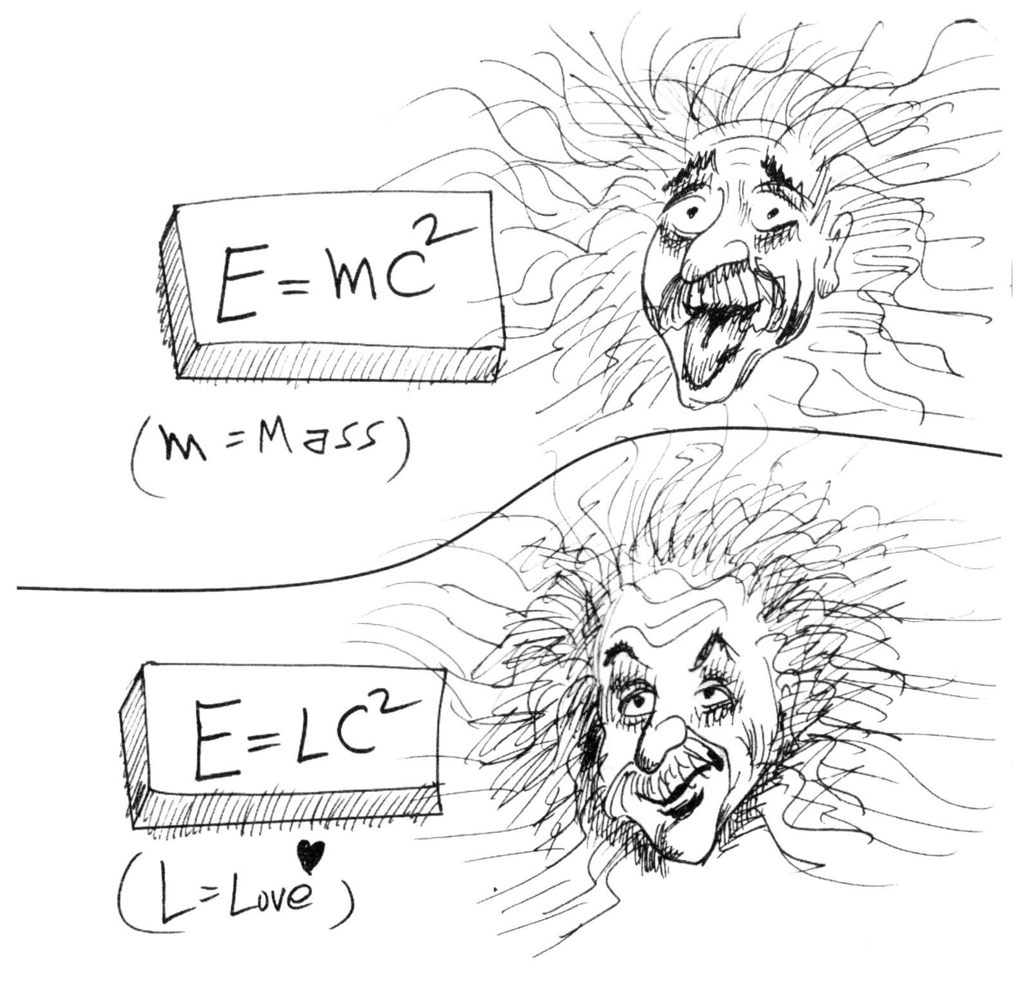

I am rattled easily by past tormentors of the workplace. Seeing their images suffocates me. I want to learn to feel a sense of equanimity ... how to do that?... I want to feel complete in myself ... as I did when I watched the sunset settle over the moat in Gadakhai ... our beloved Killa Fort ... with you.

My Bou calling us home...

"It is evening.....come home."

Then her experimental delicious snacks ... some bought ..some homemade....

"Come home"...

I return home hand in hand with you...

The evening will go on .... and we catch the magic of the times on our palms...

My childhood was not perfect...

And I was driven by demons in my head then too

But my time with you was always perfect....

The fragrance of cinnamon and nutmeg on baked apples in your NY home....

Heal my dearest heal!

Bizi

Letter 18

Affection, Addiction and Cinco de Mayo

– Sangita, New York,
5 May 2020

"Mama, you have an addiction."

"What is that?"

"You have an addiction to give affection".

"What do you mean by that?"

"Every time I am around you have to stroke my hair, or my face, or throw kisses, as a result, I have to run and hide."

A conversation between a $12^{1/2}$-year-old child with his mother. Pretty soon, this for me will end – the boy will develop a grotesque voice, the sweetness of childhood will be lost. I have been through this journey before and I know where this road leads to.

Corona fear has led us to prepare homemade Corona fighting "beer" – I have washed down my throat with warm water, lime, turmeric, grated ginger and cayenne pepper. I have drunk three glasses of it and two cups of hot tea. They say this is the best way to fight this virus – not to let it settle on the throat but to take it into the stomach where the acid will eat it up before it can proliferate. The magic potion plus the magic of your prayers have both conjoined and worked.... Thank you for your prayers – again, your prayers work powerfully for me and my critters.

Ah, Mr. Rogers! I grew up with him, over here in NY. I used to watch him daily as a 24-year-old until the show ended. I used to like the simplicity of the show and his soft-spoken ways – he reminded me of my father. I talk to my father daily, thanks to the lockdown. We speak for a few minutes – his voice is therapeutic and I know it is transient. One day I will hear it only inside my heart, and that may sound unbearable, but I am getting prepared for it.

Tess Dobashi, a Japanese friend of mine, returned to Tokyo, with her 2 children, just so, her children can experience witnessing old age and death. I am talking about my friendship that happened 23 years ago, with this interesting girl. Tess wrote many letters after returning to Japan. I placed those letters in a special place and unable to find them now – so many nests we have changed since she has been gone.... But I can still feel her through the beautiful Japanese pottery she left with me – her own, that she could not carry on that long journey back home. All these relationships with parents, friends ... all transient – they come and they leave – we have to carry on with their memories burning within us. Let that not bring us down. Love should not bring us down – it should give us wings to fly.

Mr. Rogers had demons within him – his name is not free from controversies as well ... that he prevented Francois Clemmons, a black artist, from coming out of the closet and expressing himself as gay, as that would have affected his show negatively. "I love the way you are" philosophy did not ring true in reality. No one is immune to the demons within. We simply have to work it out and try to give this life a chance.

"Mama would you rather be hungry or would you rather be thirsty?" Sachin asks me now, while I am typing up this letter to you.

"I would rather be hungry" I answer – the answer has to be thought out within 45 seconds and presented and then a discussion usually follows after. Today he has let me be. He knows I am writing to you. He had said – "Publish these letters and an apt title for it will be "PANDEMIC LETTER 5".

'Why?' I had asked and was told "Because that is a catchy title! It will garner attention."

You and I were neighbours once upon a time – Mr. Rogers had said *"Imagine what our real neighborhoods would be like if each of us offered, as a matter of course, just one kind word to another person."*

You and I have been kind towards each other ... it has come naturally – no effort made. You and I have always sat on a rock overlooking the water – in Cuttack and in New York. We have dreamt many things together without competing – we never felt the need for it....

Nanda aunty comes to mind. Today is Cinco de Mayo here – celebrating Mexico – its colorful tradition and culture. Aunty would have sewn vibrant coloured skirts and dresses for her children to wear with ornate hats and would have thrown a large feast, inviting all of us to come together.

Let us come together....

Sangita

Letter 19

The Immigrant Bride

– Bijayalaxmi, New Delhi,
6-9 May 2020

Between thirst and hunger
Many questions disappeared
These days they coalesced
Into a pandemic stupor
You are 24 years old
With your lotus eyes shining with dreams.

Newly minted marriage...
Armed with a notebook full of your mother's familiar Indian recipes...
To cook in an unfamiliar New York Apartment...
Hanging clothes on a washing line
Fragrance of a synthetic spring
Lingering in the strange cold air
A stranger returns home
To you and you set your table
To welcome him there...
Telephone to home then raspy and precious...

Frank Rogers smiling at you
From the Boxy TV set
Reminding you of your father And these days they
Collapsed into each other...

Snow shoveling and car parking
Warm summers and cold winters
Passion for your exotica mingle
With snigger from others...
You are all Indian in a New York Street
Comfortable in your lazy sexy sassy self...
Battles within and outside...
Lighted times in dim libraries
Dark souls in bright hospitals
Your healing love giving life
Children...lovers ...husband...
Cats...trees and birds....
All bad times that we face
Is a map to our best selves
Your home is a collage
Of sewn misty forgotten dreams and
Loving acceptance...
Yes, Mausi and Bou...
Are sitting on a joyous cloud
Mausi is stitching the wounds in them

And Bou is sewing laces around it
Even in pain beauty is a must
Darken your eyes with kohl
And laugh with your mouth open
Surrounded by the tenacious
Love of disagreeable children
The stranger is now your home
And these days they are yours
For your complete acceptance....

Love
Bizi

Letter 20

Of Meera Bai and the Short Tresses

– Sangita, New York,
13 May 2020

Maoli meowed in the morning to wake me up – my natural alarm clock in case I sleep a wee bit more than usual. I had wanted my dream to continue, but it ended.

In the dream, you had a short bob and your rest of the hair lay on my living room table, like a horse's mane, neatly kept. I ask you, "why did you cut your hair off?"

You replied, "I will be in NY for a while, Rajesh and I have come on an assignment". Then you went on to say "But my hair was my clothing to cover myself, how will I cover myself now?"

I look at you and ask "Will you donate your hair to the American Cancer Society?"

You reply "I am looking into organizations".

I look at your face – A Jackie Kennedy hairstyle, you look very different and naked, neck down without hair.

My thoughts then proceed to "What will Uncle do without you alone in Delhi"? That leads to another thought "How will my in-laws survive alone in old age? ...my father is alone as well without my mother "

I look at you again – you are still expressing concern about exposure of your gentle form. Your long neck is exposed and your face looks wider and more expressive – earlier the hair had taken all the credit, the face is exposed now like a

Jackson Pollock art – the hair on the table ebony and the bobbed hair on the head salt and pepper....

"Meow ... Meow" – two words break the dream.

"Has Maoli ever pooped on your arms, whenever you have held her?" asks Sachin, seeing me spring from the bed.

"What a question to ask Sachin! and that too first thing in the morning?"

"The way you squish her, I always wonder " I see him blowing his funny away.

Meera Bai – I only read about her as a child in an Amar Chitra Katha (a popular graphic storybook in India) – Your research on her and your knowledge about her is vast. I gathered that from your academic writing. You are a Meera in many ways – yearning for the perfect form in the beloved that can only be found in the formless.... You have an incredible talent in writing prose and poetry – and you let your hair hang down....

Today I have been under the weather – ate the wrong kind of food for my body for the past 3 days and this small deviation has led to acidity and high blood pressure. Kentucky Fried Chicken is something that does not agree with me. I ate one piece each for the past 3 days....

I must be mindful and not commit the same mistake.

Love and blessings

Sangita

LETTER 21

Rabindranath Tagore and the Offer of Songs

– Bijayalaxmi, New Delhi,
13-17 May 2020

Your lovely email of May 13, 2020, deserved an immediate answer. But somewhere the words got stuck in me. If I was Maoli I guess I would have written brightly coloured meows to you with a cat paw but I am just a human being trying to be relevant in this COVID driven lockdown bursting at its seams telling us about been productive by working from home.

Ah, my dearest, the only way I can imagine how I would look with short hair is by seeing you.... Jackie Kennedy and Audrey come to mind for sure when I see you ... white women with long necks.... I wonder why we feel so like them is it their vulnerability? Or their unnamed pain....

You do see me more than anyone can.....it is indeed lovely to be seen like that ... for being seen for who I am....

So the words have finally come to me and I strive to hold them together so that I can write to you...

I was reading Rabindranath Tagore's *Gitanjali* such simple and brilliant lines believe Yeats read it on his way in a train and wept inconsolably with its beauty and then immediately recommended it for the Nobel Prize. Nandini, a brilliant friend, told me this. Suddenly, I felt nostalgic for a train journey with you holding a copy of the *Gitanjali* in my hands weeping with its lines. I am no Yeats but one does not have to be a great writer to be moved by a piece of brilliant writing....

Your wedding anniversary pictures move me immensely. Your care and effort to reenact a photograph of your youth fills me with a bittersweet longing for many things that could have been.

The lockdown in Delhi has been extended till 31 May. Rajesh is going to the office and my work hours are lengthening with pressures for all kinds of data as well as a sort of mad competition to conduct online education and seminars. Webinars, they are called. I feel lost trying to hold it all together. My domestic help Shobha has returned and supports me in the household chores. She is sweet and pretty a young prim and proper lady from the Uttarkhand hills the fresh mountain sunlight still radiating from her face. She has a beautiful 18-year daughter going to college and a younger son in school. Her husband who worked in the packaging industry has no earnings now due to it closing down. She takes preventive measures wearing masks and gloves. She wants better opportunities for her children. She was saving her money for her children's education but the last two months she has been the sole breadwinner and the money is only for bare survival. She works in two homes for six hours in total and gets 22 thousand rupees in total. She is very grateful I paid her for the last two months (which was her right yet it seems to her I did a good deed.. such is the paradox of unorganised work). She is here for 3 hours. Her dignity in her work is amazing. It is nice to have her support but I do get worried about Nana. He is 78 years old. What if something happens to him because I could not manage all the work by myself ... as if Shobha is the only way for the disease to enter our make-believe bubble. We could give her the disease too. Rajesh is also out for work and groceries. He may bring the disease. Shobha has a whole family to support. Her life is as precious as ours. I tried my best to unlearn my prejudices and privileges by constantly questioning myself. Still a long way ... still not there yet.... But always striving to be aware...

We are all like Parikshit of the Mahabharata building walls around us and not stepping out because our horoscopes say a snake would kill us. And yet the snake enters as a worm in a vegetable and kills him.

Such a powerful tale. A bright and unique friend of mine Bharati made this reference in an article she wrote on the madness of the lockdown.

We cannot escape our destiny…

Death ... marriage ... birth ... all predestined ... all framed like pictures in a photo frame on a mantelpiece ... re-enacted over and over again...

I wish I was Meerabai moving to the strings of my own passion... I wish I was...

But I am not destined for it.

Yet I hold your hand against all that destiny has done to separate us...

I will do so forever...

This ... I choose by my passion for our simple and brilliant friendship. A Gitanjali of our own....

"The best stories are not always written ... they are felt in our hearts."

Love
Bizi

LETTER 22

Ferdinand and Gitanjali

– Sangita, New York,
17 May 2020

Webinars
Minars
Both towering
Over you
The Delhi Sky
Looks blue
It has taken a new hue
Grey skies are gone
Until Corona
hangs strong.

What is a better alternative for humans – clear skies and lungs or jobs to feed starving mouths? Is there a middle ground to all of this? Can it ever be reached, where nature, animals, humans all can coexist without starving and getting exploited?

Is ambition the root cause of all evil?

In 1936, Mr. Munro Leaf had written a children's story on a legal pad – it had taken him less than an hour to write it and it is still one of the greatest children's classics of all time. It is "*The Story of Ferdinand*". It had created a great deal of controversy, when it was published and in fact, was banned in Spain and burnt in Nazi Germany – it was seen as promoting fascism and communism. It happens to be one of my favourite books that I read many times to my children before kissing them goodnight.

I happen to relate to Ferdinand well. He speaks after my heart. He is a bull that prefers to smell flowers rather than fight with other bulls. He is a content little being in his own world, even though he happens to be the strongest and largest of all bulls in Spain and could outbull (is that a word?) the mightiest of bulls, yet he prefers to remain under a cork tree and smell flowers.

You and I sitting on a rock in front of the moat – two mighty beings content smelling each other's fragrance that wafted through the air. To compete and be first was the last thing in our minds. To compete with each other never crossed our minds as well. It was a friendship beyond competition. It was possible.

Ah! Shobha, with her grace, has eased your pressures of mundane household chores at home. She reminds me of Ms. A, her name means "brave". She happens to be my colleague, who in her spare time, helps out the ultra-rich in Manhattan. She was offered a job to babysit two children. There were certain strings attached – she will be offered an apartment in Upper East Side (rent is $3,000 a month that will be paid for) and be paid $5000 weekly cash, food and sundries all will be provided by the family. Their only request was she cannot expose herself to anyone and after work she will stay inside her apartment as long as Corona continues. The other request was she cannot meet her aging father, lest he gives the infection to her and in turn, she infects the rich woman's father, who happens to be a high flying lawyer in NY ... after all, older men are more susceptible to the virus!

In the rich lady's words "I just want to make sure we do a full isolation (UGH) for the full period just to make absolutely sure. Your father hasn't been coming and going in your apartment?"

The wealthy father's life was more precious than Ms. A's father ... who is solely taken care of by her. She asked for my advice....

I simply texted "Their father is important only! And you are asked not to be around your father! It is a lot of money I know but your father and you come first.

God will provide in some other way after this situation passes. Sometimes we need to take difficult decisions in life, and after we take them, no more turning back – we must look forward with whatever we chose and make the best out of it."

In a few days she wrote back "I feel so much better since I denied taking that job. I was very stressed out. I am not going to have that much $, but I will be happy. I will be praying for you, because you are a very special person – a nurse that really cares. Thank you for everything, for being there, for your amazing energy!"

The rich and their sense of entitlement! The exploiter and the exploited!

The smog and fog of Delhi and the global stench, all reek of their breath!

Ferdinand and Gitanjali go hand in hand – both spill out the essence of life – love!

Sangita

Another Dream

– 21 May 2020

My Dearest me,

Hope things are ok in your part of the world.

I had a dream of you – we are in Disney world – a driver drove us there. And you tell me, you want to go on every ride. I look at the crowd of people and wonder whether it is safe during Corona time to be in Disney World in the first place.

Then as luck would have it, you and I separate in the mass of humanity and I do not have a cell phone to contact you – the driver is also nowhere to be found. I am wondering what to do – I keep looking for you in the maddening crowd and trying to remember if we ever made a plan and agreed upon a place to meet, in case we got lost – my dream breaks.

I spend some time musing upon my dream – what is this journey about?

Love,
Sangita

Simba

"Can you save these plants? The landscaper just ripped them out!! I have a feeling you can heal them."

The plants in question were purple pansies. The season of spring had ended and summer flowers were replacing them in front of the hospital that I worked as an HIV/AIDS nurse.

The mutilated plants were given to me with a lot of trust that I will not hurt them.

My colleagues looked at me with interest to see how I would react to such a fragile gift – the gift from a 'madman'.

"I will try my best. Thank you for trusting me." The plants were placed gently on my hands. I took care not to drop the dirt on the clinic floor on my way back to my room.

I took the pansies home and planted them on a pot in my patio. They sprang back to life and bloomed beyond expectations for a couple more months until their season really came to an end.

Every time I see pansies those words come back "Can you save these plants?"

I could save the pansies and the gift-giver but only to a certain point.

Blue and purple pansies are blooming on my patio, spring is almost melting into summer. Pretty soon they will lose their beauty and pass on to the next world. 2020 has put a standstill to the human agenda, but nature keeps bursting with life.

Sachin and I pray for Simba's leg – I hope the right leg will heal and Simba will stand strong. The most one can do is try, the outcome may not match our expectations ... so many hidden and overt variables in life.

Love love love

Sangy

Letter 23

Being Poor

– Bijayalaxmi, New Delhi,
17-21 May 2020

I am consistent in my inconsistency in replying to you. I hope you will forgive me. I say this with a smile on my face because I know you will. Imagine if all relationships were this way. What a beautiful little nugget of a poem.

I write one in reply:

New York chill
With the Indomitable Corona Will
Skyscrapers and sirens
Amalgam to a silence
With the trumping of violence
NYC and ND ... what is in a name?
Pandemic questions are the same
Who shall laugh ... who shall cry...
Who shall live ... who shall die...

Unpredictable times we live in ... Some comfort from food and books.

Some comfort from conversations with loved ones. Ferdinand ... Geetanjali ... all these writings were meant for us ... the soft-bellied middle class ...for their indulgence. So that they can feel superior and scoff the rich and feel sorry for the poor. And remain vacillating between the two...

You advised that lady well. The poor can never make an informed and empowered choice because they are worried for their everyday survival.

I feel poor when in New York. The rupee pales into a pittance in front of the machismo of the dollar. The disposability of my middle- class income becomes converted into the preciousness of a daily wager. I feel reduced ... invisible and starkly vulnerable.... colour ... clothes ... codes... I count every penny when I buy. So I guess, to some extent it is my experiential understanding of poverty. However, I know I can escape it once I return. It is only a matter of a short visit. But imagine being stuck in that zone of hopelessness. Poverty makes it difficult to choose. That is why I respect those who irrespective of all their economic burdens choose a life of labour and dignity. I do not know about myself. Maybe I would have sold my soul in these circumstances ... maybe not...

The drive seems reminiscent of our Kerala trip. The fear of not meeting each other again looms large in all of us. But hope nestles in my heart. Maybe I will take all the rides in Disney land with you....

Fantasy Island we have to create...

There was a huge cyclone in West Bengal and parts of Odisha yesterday. Unheard of velocity...

Curses galore for all, especially the poor. Prayers and love.

Your
BG

LETTER 24

New Delhi and Old York

– Sangita, New York,
21 May 2020

There is an Old Delhi and a New Delhi

But New York – will it ever become Old York?

I wonder about that as well – will I be around to see New York? I have been to New York but not New York....

These kinds of thoughts enter my head – no I have plenty of work to do - my plate is full and hands are full, but thoughts dime a dozen all the time. I let them flow and end on their own.

This is something I have realized late in life – to let thoughts flow, rather than curbing them. And if we pay full attention to our thoughts, then something magical happens – we become capable of choosing the right kind of thought and freeing ourselves from unnecessary chatter.

"What are you doing?" asks Soumya. "I am writing," I say

"I can't handle your damn pandemic letters anymore," she says. "But you have not read even one" I frown.

"You read an excerpt to me that was like 10 minutes long". She grins from ear to ear and goes her own sweet way.

Sachin giggles –

I look up to find him engrossed in his own virtual world.

"Poor" is such a subjective phenomenon ... who really is poor? Richie Rich comes to mind – "Poor little rich boy" – he was labeled both ... you in the US with Indian rupees, the Venezuelan bolivar and the Iranian rial......

I was giving away a quarter of my salary to a homeless man every month – now I feel extremely rich after his disappearance and feel mighty poor as well. He enriched my life in many ways. He had absolutely nothing material to give me but showed me a wealth of wisdom.

In the final analysis – what is wealth? Who is poor? A person with rupees, bolivars, rials or dollars?

I remember one time I was very thirsty and I had no cash on me. The man with very little of his own went to purchase water for me from the gas station – in his pocket, all he had was $1 and he spent it all on the bottle of water....

Contemplatively yours

Sangita

The Stubborn Princess

– 22 May 2020

Sabitri – The princess who fell in love with a poor man, who she chanced upon from her father's chariot, while passing through a jungle and walked into the jaws of death to bring him back into the mortal world....

Today happens to be her day –

It is quite a significant day, in the time Corona ....

Sabitri's anklets tinkling still rings in the fertile fields of my mind – a story that I read over and over again, growing up in Odisha, from an Amar Chitra Katha.

I had shared the story last night with Satwick while he paid a visit to the kitchen looking for food. I had said to him "Tomorrow is Sabitri and mama will take a break."

"What is Sabitri? Isn't she your friend from Cuttack?" "She is named after Sabitri, Sabitri is. "

He listened to the story with interest without interruption and commented "An interesting concept. Ok, what then shall we do tomorrow – who will cook food?"

"Sabitri and her giants can eat pizza," I said.

I decided to share this story early in the morning with Sachin. He came into my bed like a lumbering bear and flopped by my side."

"Today is Sabitri, Sachin."

"What is Sabitri?"

"Once upon a time. .."

"Can you get to the point?"

"There lived a princess who was going through a jungle on a chariot with her dad and saw a man and fell in love with him and after returning home told her father she will marry him and no one else." I rushed through this whole sentence as if running a 100-meter dash, no pauses.

"Psychopathic in my view – to be seeing some random guy in a jungle and telling her dad that she will marry him."

"The king, her dad, sent his soldiers to the forest to find the man, and they also found that he had only one year to live."

"Mama ... get to the point."

"So, they married and one year passed and he fell down while cutting wood ."

Silence from Sachin....

"Sabitri placed his head on her lap, and Yama came riding on his bull."

"Who is Yama?"

"God of death – he came to take Satyaban with him and Sabitri started following him."

"Where?"

"To the gates of death and she kept walking and she was wearing anklets and they went ting ting ting."

"Okkkkkkk is that the end?"

"No ... Yama seeing so much devotion in her told her he will grant her 3 wishes."

"Did she wish to bring him back to life?"

"She was not given that choice. With the exception of that, she could ask 3 things and her wish would be granted – her first wish was that her in-laws will be able to see again, her second wish was her in- laws will be given back their kingdom, that rightfully belonged to them – Yama said TATHASTU and asked her what her final wish was?"

"Hmm"

"Sabitri wished to give birth to 100 children, maybe 1000 ... I don't remember now. And Yama said TATHASTU. Yama started walking and told her to go back to the mortal world as all her wishes have been granted."

"And"

"Sabitri said 'How can I go back without my husband?" "What do you mean?" Yama asked.

"For my third wish to come true, I have to have my husband beside me, otherwise how can I be a mother to 100 children?"

Yama could see that she had outsmarted him and returned her husband's soul into his body and Sabitri and Satyaban lived happily ever after.

Married women from Odisha observe Sabitri, so their husbands could live a very long life. Today I am planning on observing it, so we can eat fruits and maybe I don't have to cook and just take it easy."

"This Bull Guy is kinda stupid! – that's all I can say mama. And my question to you is, wasn't adoption around then? What about single parenthood? What if the husbands are abusive, why pray for their long life?"

Mother-child session ended – the day needed to begin with a shower and washing the fruits and slicing them and offering them to Sabitri.

Breakfast was a fruit fest of blueberries, strawberries, mangoes, cherries and bananas. A sister in law of mine seeing the photo posted on WA wrote, "There were no blueberries and cherries in Savitri's forest!! No Strawberries either. So only mangoes are the only fruits you can eat."

"Wondering if mangoes were there as well ... so I drank tea and ate gajjas."

My Dearest me – the wind chimes go ting-ting-ting – I am sitting outside and writing this letter to you. I purchased a new wind chime today – it is a red bird, with a yellow beak and 4 red-colored crystals are hanging down from a piece of thread in the middle. When the wind is blowing, its wings are fluttering and it chimes - ting ting ting. And the other one was a gift from Dylan, Soumya's friend – he had rescued it from a garbage bin and had handed it to Soumya and had told her "It is for your mother, she will appreciate it."

– 29 May – 3 June 2020

The Short-horned grasshoppers

The Wuhan bats

The Pangolins

Cyclone Amphan

Cyclone Nisarga

The Minnesota polices.

One thing in common in all of the above – a death.

Death of human beings in various ways – through a disease, natural disaster, second-degree murder.

America is shuddering because of the murder of a black man by a white man in the most inhuman way; a physical death captured on cell phone cameras. That is in my part of the world.

In your part of the world, media is showing the horrific ways of America – racism, colorism, discrimination....

What is racism?

What is colorism?

I faced both growing up in India – a brown girl. dirty colored girl, muddy colored girl, dark, colored, black, beautiful but – unique beauty but – sharp features but –

There always existed a 'but' growing up. It was always a concern of the women folk – my colour. It was something to be addressed, otherwise a problem later on with the marriage.

"Fair and Lovely Creams", "Turmeric paste", "Sandalwood", "Milk and chickpea flour", all suggested to alleviate my 'darkness' by the womenfolk.

Mother never paid heed to these advices. She would say, "You have a sweet complexion. Your face is your fortune, take care of it. I neglected myself, you must not." I did not listen to her. I never did, except once in her lifetime. She had visited me in 2004 and had said "You will make a very good nurse."

Coming to the United States I seemed 'colourless' in the eyes of the West. All the colours of Indians mingled into oneness and accepted as simply an American of Indian origin.

George Floyd was a black man whose murder was recorded by cell phones.

Countless women get murdered for their colour – there is no physical death to record – it happens within - goes unnoticed.

I happen to be alive – a lucky survivor!

Love
Sangy

Letter 25

Aurobindo and Eternity of Soul

– Bijayalaxmi, New Delhi,
22-29 May 2020

Aurobindo, the great revolutionary who turned philosopher, social reformer and saint, wrote a magnum opus on the Sabitri. He elucidated that the story is a deep philosophical metaphor about the eternity of the soul. It emphasizes love, discipline, truth and devotion to lengthen our lives and sustain our life sources. Satyavan symbolised truth, i.e., life is impermanent and Savitri's love, and for a better word emotional intelligence, can bring us close to life's eternal spring. He referred to it as the highest embodiment of the reality of life. In other words, the truth of human life is mortality and by love and devotion, we can struggle against our lower selves and conquer it by finding our way and evolving to our spiritual destiny and avoiding early mortality through divine love.

The stories of human lovers as you can see are transient. The story of the divine soul is eternal.

My workdays are prolonged due to the uncertainty of how examinations are going to finally unfold during this period. I really have no answers to that but I have to be part of discussions to decide that!

I also get tied up with writing and preparing for presentations. So my day is divided over working from home and cooking and worrying about Simba. His aging is painful to watch. far more painful than my own. He is only 14 in human years and in his 80s in dog years. His eyes are glassy now and he has started limping too. His slow gait ... his inability to run and his difficulty in sleeping, all disturb me no end.

The 60 days of my home stay where I have not stepped out at all has made me realise that I am essentially a loner. I did not know that about myself. I realise I can spend the rest of my life writing, reading and just engaging with 2 or 3 people and Simba. Of course, groceries have to be bought and Simba has had 4 trips to the hospital which Rajesh has managed well till now. For that, I am eternally grateful.

Delhi is under the throes of a curse. We have bizarre weather with unimaginable heat and then storms and rain showers. There are reports and warnings of a possible locust infestation (already arrived in Jaipur devastating crops there) and we have experienced a number of mild intensity earthquakes. Today also there was one but I did not feel it.

However, I wonder what will the future say about this period?

'It was the best of times, it was the worst of times' so said Charles Dickens of the French Revolution.

I think when our future generation refers to this period of human history they will say that. The conflicts for human resources, the genophobic hatred, especially against people of colour, migrants, refugees the violence against women and children and the terrifying devastation of our environmental resources. The Covid19 is an amalgamation of all that. It is us ... mutating virus, hybrid from a half- human and half-animal.

This obsessive cleaning reminds me of Macbeth. We are all washing our hands of the blood of all whom we annihilated.

Sachin and your mantra so deeply and truly spoken will definitely cure him.

You are the saviour of pansies

And cats and waifs and dogs

And my ever broken heart.

Hope and prayers my dearest me ... the lilting songs you sing to Maoli, bring good tidings.

I hope Simba recovers soon so that I can sing and dance with abandon with you.

I suddenly remember right now the terrible song of our childhood from a Hindi movie sung by the great Usha Uthup with her husky sultry western touch and her heavy Kanjivaram sarees...

Ramba ho ...

Samba ho...

Mein nachun...

Tum nachon...

Jitni hi Zindagi utni hi ... something.... something... Till

we live let our souls dance....

We will dance to this in a retro virtual party soon...

Or do a Travolta on Saturday night.

See you soon...

Smilingly yours
Bizi

LETTER 26

Breathless in the Hybrid of Networks

– Bijayalaxmi, New Delhi,
6 June 2020

I am sitting in my dining chair.

Now my office work from a home chair

Plumped up by two brilliantly orange cushions ... sold to me by a toothless chequered face lady in the Dilli Haat...

Examining the doomsday scenario

Of exotic names

Storms and birds

Creatures of nature

Weaving their music

Of death around us

The laptop camera

Is my eye to the world now

I stare disagreeably at it

I am now a hybrid of networks

Technical and human.

Colours of rhapsody on the kurta I am wearing. I see a tiny bug with florescent wings settled happily on the vivid yellow banana in front of me. These colours that break people into categories and finally unleash deep discrimination and violence.

I cannot understand how passionately racist human beings can be? The death of George Floyd under the knee of a policeman. His last words "I cannot breathe" echoes around us. So many times these kinds of repression and prejudices make me feel that I cannot breathe anymore.

Then your experience of being traumatized by the presence or absence of a pigment angers me further... To me you are all shades of the rainbow and the peacock feathers. I do not know how no one sees that ... the magic of all your colours! I feel a sense of helplessness and hopelessness for this suffering that is meted for centuries all over the world ... in our home in the name of colours and shades.

I am so glad that you found your magic cloak of invisibility in the U.S. The irony, of course, is not lost on me. Your own family treats you this way and the land which is the bastion of racism, you found acceptance there. Hannah Arendt, the famous German-Jewish philosopher, refers to prejudice which can and has led to genocide as "the banality of evil". Evil is not a strategic and monstrous grand plan ... it is premised on absurdities and practiced by the most average and ordinary human beings. She spoke this in the context of Eichmann who carried out the word of Hitler to the hilt and ordered the massacre of thousands of Jews. Arendt, who was following the trial of Eichmann in Jerusalem after the second world war ended, found to her surprise that Eichmann's physical appearance looked unassuming and harmless and listless and clueless. The sweet auntie, the pretty mom-in-law, the friendly neighbour are all a banal army of the evil. Is banal a word, I wonder?...

But I guess these combinations of letters are to delineate it a meaning and I am sure you have understood. Incidentally, Arendt was not so critical of colonization or racism in other countries. She was more reflective of the Nazi excesses against Jews because that was her life...

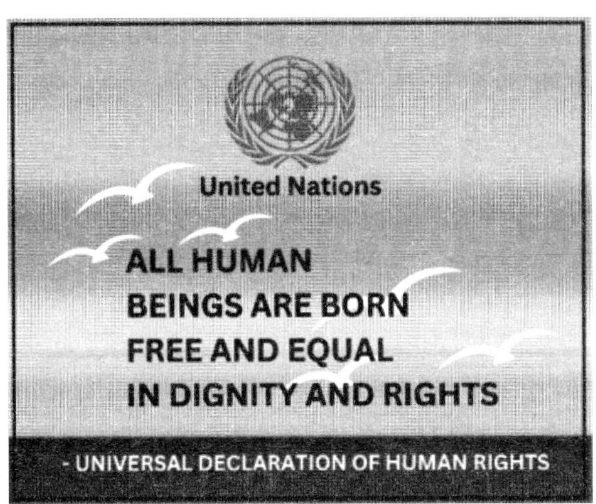

We understand the suffering we face but once we extrapolate from there about suffering in general, we learn the true meaning of human existence is to question and discard such stereotypes and prejudices.

Yesterday Ashee said something interesting. She said when the perpetrator has a visible face – like a policeman we attack it with all our might but then there are phantom perpetrators whom we cannot annihilate. We need to understand that. Once we face the phantom then maybe there can be hope for change...

While your streets are exploding with protestors ... our streets are filling up with the coronavirus patients. It is getting really worrying now and I hope and pray things improve. Spring brings new colours

.... I hope the anticipation of your spring in our blazing summer will bring the much-needed healing from this disease of breathlessness of Covid19 and colour, caste, creed, class discrimination.

Breathe ... spring is around the turn...

Breathe ... we will find the radiant sun...

Love and light
Bizi

LETTER 27

Phantom and the Colour of Beauty

– Sangita, New York,
9 June 2020

The "Phantom Perpetrators" – they reside within and around us. The little lady – your daughter, in the Big Apple, knows it too well – the color of melanin. She too happens to be a melanin queen, like me. Thoughts are 'phantom perpetrators' as well – the observer needs to observe the thoughts that reside within and let it flow out and turn to vapor; thoughts must not be allowed to color the mind!

Most animals are color blind, so they say. They can only see black and white. Our cat Maoli is black and white and sees in black and white – her behavior towards us is black and white as well. There are no shades of grey – either she behaves or misbehaves – there are no pretensions of love; when she smiles, she smiles – it is not a veil. She reminds me of our mothers. Our mothers, transparent and treacherous in their tirades towards us. We got clawed and bit by their stark honesty and their irrepressible courage to speak out their minds. They raised us to be strong women to face the battle of life.

In these trying times of Corona, Cyclones and Colorism, let the power of our mothers' love flow within us. Let not the Three C's cow us down. My dearest me – I see you in me. I am you in me in you. If only humanity sees it similarly!

COVID-19 is finally slowing down in New York City. The Big Apple finally reopened yesterday – an exciting moment for New Yorkers. They say "one apple a day, keeps the doctor away". The Big Apple survived, thanks to the millions of frontline workers who placed themselves in the jaws of death to keep the Apple alive! Three CHEERS to them!

I pray for Delhi to deal and duel with COVID and defeat the deadly virus. Delhi always has stood strong!

COVID-19 and soul-searching letters exchanged between you and me - pandemic letters ... 29 of them? I have lost count ... let them continue.

Love
Sangy

– 24 June 2020

I saw her son while I was coming out of the car. He was standing in front of her house.

I asked, “How is Sonia?”

He did not reply.

I asked again, “How is your mother?”

His face had a deadpan look.

I waited for my question to be answered.

He said "My mother is no more. She passed away in March. Not from COVID. She had many surgeries done but it was her heart that gave up. “March!” And she lived right across the road from my nest, on the other side; the side where the houses cost 2 million dollars. I stopped dead on my tracks. The “papdi chaat” on my hand shook. We had just returned from our weekly trip to buy Indian groceries from Patel Brothers, and had stopped at Surya Restaurant – “Mama, could you get me 'chaat' from Surya, I am longing for some?” my daughter Soumya had asked.

Sonia! The tiny lady with diamonds sparkling on her ears and fingers. Her impeccably dressed $4^{1/2}$ feet frame that radiated with wealth and vitality. Her wavy blonde hair shining like gold in the sun – a short, chic bob. Her perfume wafting through the air. Her luxury car waiting in the driveway, her husband waiting patiently to take her on a car ride. She would always make him wait and talk to me. Every time I passed by her house she would stop me and give me a hug. I would say “Mrs. Ulrich, you look so beautiful!” She would reply “My dear it is all makeup, all show, you are beautiful – look at you – nothing on your face – that is real beauty. You are going to pick up your son, aren't you? go, my dear, I will not stop you.” She always scurried around her front lawn, planting flowers and watering them. Sonia had a tiny wagon, where she kept her gardening tools and dirt to spruce up her garden space. She would put her wide sun hat on her glistening hair and work for hours on the Sun. She always made sure to prepare a pot of flowers for me and place it on my front porch. Flowers that were as radiant as her and aromatic! We would talk of my parents and her mother, who lived in Canada; a fiercely independent woman touching 100. Sonia would break down in front of me. "Oh, my mother, she lives so far away. I can understand your pain, my dear. And your mother's pain. My mother does not want to move in with me. She loves her independence. So must your mother." I would hug her and she would cling gently onto me. "Mrs. Ulrich, your perfume smells so subtle and fesh."

"My dear, wait for a minute, won't you?". With a half-used perfume bottle on her hand, she would scurry back to me. "Use it my dear, it will suit you more, you are young."

Sonia was not my biological mother but understood me well. She and I shared an intimate bond. She visited me only once, when Sachin was born and my parents had come. She sat with us like family. Her life was busy, with her husband and her children and grandchildren, who lived in Long Island and Manhattan.

The day her husband passed, she stopped coming out of her house. I did not see her for a long time. The snow never ceased to melt – it was a stubborn winter a couple of years back when snowstorms were aplenty; we had lost count. When I met her again during one of my daily walks, I saw her in a wheelchair pushed around by a heavy – set black woman on her cell phone. I could not recognize Sonia. I had to peer closely and saw a pale-faced ghost of a woman straddled onto the wheelchair. I exclaimed "Mrs. Ulrich!". She looked at me with glassy eyes. "My dear! yes, it is me." She asked the home health aide to stop and wait. The woman was still busy on her phone jabbering away. She paid no mind to her frail employer.

"Look at me, my dear. I have no make-up on. You are seeing me as I am. My dear, you are still a beauty." Sonia's ear lobes were empty, her hair grey, frizzy and uncombed. Her face ashen. Tears rolled down her eyes. "My dear, my husband is no more. We were married for a long time. He was not a doctor like your husband but he was a hardworking man. He built everything for me." She clasped my hand and clung to my frame like the old times. All that was left of Sonia were her soft warm palms and her gentle smile. Her smile reached her eyes and I saw them sparkle like her diamonds used to on her ear lobes. "How is your father, my dear? He must miss your mother. I know how it feels my dear. Give your father my love."

Her thick Jewish accent still rings in my ears. "Give your father my love." Her empty perfume bottle that I had held on to for years, I threw it out recently during one of my cleaning sprees to declutter the nest. "Dostadning" had led me to throw away the perfume bottle. "Dostadning" a gentle art of Swedish death cleaning in order to free oneself and one's family from a lifetime of clutter.

All I have of her now is her memories. And yes – a cat grooming brush with a neon green handle and a bowl decorated with imprints of fish and smiling cats with whiskers on them. She had gifted our cat Maoli, during our first month of moving into our nest. That was 19 years ago! "My dear, my cat is no more, perhaps your cat will make use of the brush and bowl."

Love
Sangy

Letter 28

Monali's Departure

– Bijayalaxmi, New Delhi,
23 August 2020

Dearest Sangita

The news of Monali's passing from this world stilled life around me. I was aware of her battling her major illness with courage and humour in the way only Monali could. Yet the fact that she was gone forever left me bereft. Her life of 48 years was miraculous and unique. It was intertwined with both of ours by a series of coincidences. She was the daughter of my parents' friends and she was related to you by marriage since she was your husband's cousin.

Her parents were our neighbours in the Delhi Government colony homes. My bond with Monali strengthened during this period. We shared many things in common. She was the eldest child in her family just as I was. We both shared notes on dealing with our younger sisters. We loved them and they exasperated us! We were both hopelessly clumsy and it bonded us well.

Monali was full of quirky stories. She cheered me up when my mother passed away ... she always hid her own struggles well. She was exceptionally bright and pursued her dreams with a rare drive and passion unlike any other person I had known. Whether it was her PhD or poetry Monali excelled in it all. When Ashee was born Monali and Geetu (soul sister and neighbour) were her Godmothers in every way. Ashee's childhood was lit because of her presence in it.

When her world turned upside down with the untimely passing away of her younger sister followed by her own divorce, Monali held her own pain incandescently. She never shared her pain when I met her she regaled me with happy stories and fed me exotic dishes that she had learnt to prepare... It was as if she did not want me to be unhappy or burdened by her sorrow... Such compassion and strength is rare as rare can be.

She was a brilliant professor who carved a niche in her chosen university in France ...I met her last in her sister Pinky's marriage. She was struggling to walk but as always was beautifully dressed and kept us all laughing with her self deprecatory humour! It was later when their father abandoned their mother that I came to know of the seriousness of her health condition. During the pandemic her mother, Rama Aunty, moved to France to bring her back to India. But Monali as always did not want to trouble anyone... She left this worldly abode quietly one evening ... dissolving into the air in the land she had chosen to work.... I feel she must be traversing in another world, pursuing her dreams, regaling people with her stories and spreading joy to all...

I hold on to a happy memory – all of us sitting around on her bed in their house in Ravindra Nagar, Delhi where you came to stay with them during your visit and we were giggling away over her jokes and the fritters she had cooked for us.... Her beautiful, innocent face glowing with the truth of who she was. She was our own unique angel... She is our own unique angel....

BIZI

Poem for Monali

Sweet Bird

Flutter your wings

Fly far away

Here fake flowers bloom

Feigning freedom

Sweet Bird

Look yonder

Fools resting their heads

On jagged thorns

Fly far away

Cry no more!

For the ones left behind

Where does a sad thought go?

Let it not settle within

Let molten lava flow

Tears let them fall

Let them roll out streaming

Screaming of freedom

Every teardrop meets its ocean

One day

Some day

Somewhere

Sangita Misra, August 24, 2020

Letter 29

Distance and Dreams

– Sangita, New York,
28 August 2020

Dearest Me

Since Tuesday, my work has begun in school. First thing that struck me is the social distancing. Here people right away grab and hug and kiss – everyone stayed away – they blew kisses and if they smiled, I could not see the curve of their lips. In some, like my principal, I could see the glint in her eyes, when she saw me. She is a Sagittarian like me; I can sense her vibes.

The janitor limped towards me and showed me his swollen ankle. He is not my responsibility, but seeing him in distress, I let him sit on a chair and I bandaged his ankle to provide support. I told him not to report to work, until the ankle healed. He said he could not call out since it was our first day of returning to work. The janitor is well loved in the school. His physique is carved perfectly with muscles rippling and a magnificent chest. He also has a kind heart inside since he donated a lot of his clothes to me to take for Jack. Both have the same height and gait. The difference between G the janitor and Jack the unemployed is the former lacks the latter's self-confidence. It may sound ironic, but it is true, the way Jack strides this earth, one may think, he owns the piece of earth he treads on. Whereas G works very hard – he has the janitor's job full time and then works as a construction worker in the night in Manhattan. I asked him why he does not go back to school and study, because after awhile, it will be tough for him to take upon so much physical load. He said he wanted to become a nurse but could not handle the course curriculum. He quit after a semester.

At work, I sit alone in my room, since there are no children, no visitors yet. But there is Ms. Ann.

Ms. Ann comes into my room in the pretext of washing her hands. First two days she went on a brisk walk with me – she has very long legs, trying to keep up with her is a huge problem for me. Yet I huffed and puffed by her side. She trusts me with her thoughts and expresses it without fear of being judged. She has four important men in her life; an aging father, a husband, a lover and a man she is in love with. She is unable to decide what to do, since all four play an integral part in her life. When she gallops by my side, I am expected to listen and share pearls of wisdom. Whatever I share is like nectar from heaven. She says, just listening to my voice calms her down and that she loves to be around me.

Once I reach home, innumerable chores wait. Tonight I have decided to let them be – I felt like writing to you instead. I felt like being around you.

Love

Sangy

LETTER 30

Achilles Heel

– Bijayalaxmi, New Delhi,
3 September 2020

Dearest Dearest Sangita

Good Morning from this side of the globe...

Your emails have brought me some unexpected joy in my otherwise mundane life like sighting a full moon in a cloudy night sky. Receiving endorsements for the manuscript is indeed heartwarming. But in a way my joy came more from the fact that it delighted you and re-energised your spirit of trust and faith in people you care about. I was worried since publication is replete with many rejections and delays and I wanted you to be shielded from all of it. You are right. We are over thinking the delays and intermittent breaks.

We always tend to overthink about such things.

Your school janitor reminded me of the Greek mythology of Achilles Heel.

As you know Achilles, a central figure in Greek mythology, was the son of the mortal Peleus, who served as the king of the Myrmidons, and Thetis, a Nereid or sea nymph. Renowned as the greatest warrior among the troops led by Agamemnon during the Trojan War, Achilles played a pivotal role in the epic conflict. According to Homer, Achilles was raised by his mother Thetis. An additional non-Homeric tale recounts that, as a child, Thetis immersed Achilles in the waters of the River Styx, rendering him invulnerable, with the exception of his heel—held by Thetis—now famously known as the "Achilles' heel."

We are all vulnerable in some ways. The good janitor with his physical fitness, his integrity and commitment to his work, his generosity and empathy for others has one weakness. His lack of confidence to strive to be an equal. The work hierarchy and the importance of retaining a secure job in order to support his family makes his confidence shrink. When we have something to lose then we are less confident in person. Yet there is the inner confidence to struggle against the odds.

Jack's Achilles Heel is his inability to return to the rituals of the world of work. He is not confident of being accepted as himself or who he was before drugs and disease robbed him of his basic human dignity. Now he has nothing to lose. He faces the fear of immediate death every day. So life by itself is his biggest conquest. So every day he feels he has conquered death.

Ann with her mischievous spirit breaking each rule in the book ... her long strides in the park and her pouring out to you about her many loves. Her Achilles Heel is her openness to the pain of clarity. Two men in her intimate circle whom she cannot love. This burden of knowing what love is ... and a man whom she loves who is not her lover.

And your Achilles Heel my dearest is your empath spirit ... in a perfect world it would never have been a vulnerability. To feel for all of them as if they were you. It is your strength too. That is why they all seek you to heal. You are a healer in every sense and like all great healers you have the power of pain transference. The other heals and you take on their pain. I know that too well. I have the same Achilles Heel.

But we are both confident in a lazy way irrespective of our Achilles Heel ... there is a lot we have to lose. So therefore our confidence is indeed the most powerful. It is the confidence of the butterfly ... touching everyone's life ... knowing life's ephemerality ... yet ready to fit into every part of it's natural order.

Every life ... each life may empathy be our Achilles heel.

Love you
Bizi

LETTER 31

The Intermission of Compensatory Memory

– Bijayalaxmi, New Delhi,
5 May 2020

Death, ideas of beauty, disease and life, all intermeshed in your story ... vividly brought out by your evocative writing. Death brings it it's own set of compensatory memory. This pandemic has brought it more news of death of near and dear ones and not all of it from Covid. A hundred years ago you and I knew nothing of death. Life stretched in front of us with all its obscure possibilities.

I wore a pale blue dress in a colour that existed in the skies of our childhood just before the monsoon rains came in. You were to visit us. There was something so pure about your visit because in my mother's eyes you were the most untainted.

She judged my friends and I did not like that and somehow it still mattered to me. The fragrance of basmati rice and fresh spices flavoured the air. My mother was preparing a feast because you were coming to visit me. The comfort of that aroma still in the air and all these years later I feel alive thinking about it.

This longing to feel alive with a love song whispering it's rhythm in my heart is what life is. Mitu's death has filled me with deep regret. Her joyous grand presence would fill up a room. No matter how many people were there in a room you would not be able to take your eyes off her. I wish I had told her that. I wish I had told her that her beauty was not skin deep ... it was soul deep. I wish I had told her that all the weight she carried from her husband's rejection of her was a useless burden that she should throw away ... that she was precious to all of us...to her parents ... her sisters ... her daughters and me. I wish I had told her that....

She had given me a set of small glass bottles filled with nuts and raisins for Diwali. I store my spices in them. Five years back ... glass bottles with turmeric powder and garam masala still nestling in my kitchen shelves. All her annual Diwali gifts are nestling somewhere in the house. And she is gone! A photograph ... a sly memory ... a bitter pain ... a happy thought ... death full of regrets ... life full of bewilderment ... the failure to cherish life when time seemed to be in abundance...

Meaningless hatred ... stigmas of colour and power spilling out like viruses all around us ... death is not enough it seems to teach us about the preciousness of life...

A self-study group of six bright precautious girls, from a class I taught political theory a year back, reach out to me every weekend to discuss some of the less mentioned women writers within the political theory traditions. We discussed Alexandra Kollantai today. She was an ambassador of Feminist Socialism and a proponent of free love.

She was critiqued for her ideas on sexuality. She was seen as advocating promiscuity. But she was not. She was just talking about equal love and solidarity.

It is sad how these great women were marginalized and reduced to footnotes in the history of the ideologies which they represented. Marxism, liberalism and socialism.

We will also discuss J.K Rowling's critique of the transgender issues and the outrage she generated with it.

Rowling is white and Cisgender and I feel she seemed a little shrill there. My students smile. I mean I think they do ... they have been understood. It is all there is. We should just understand the other. We may not agree on everything. But we can try to understand at least. They also listen to me and try to understand me. This class is a social experiment on an equal classroom where there is no judgment and no grades ... no talking down ... no power equations. They decide whom to teach and we engage with the thinkers. They initiate the class and I join in. Everyone has 10 minutes, including me. They send the reading list. We keep adding to it.

The future of classrooms can be like this perhaps. We are learning to be better people.

We will be reading Kimberly Crenshaw, the black feminist, who has provided the theory of intersectionality. I think I will read to them this letter of yours.

You are no giant ... a delicate fragile figure, but yes, you have an enormous generous love-filled heart.

Covid is spreading like wildfire here in Delhi. Deaths, disease, deprivation and debates are the keywords here.

I know New York is better but the U.S, on the whole, is replete with the same Ds as Delhi.

Prayers for the pandemic to end.
To self-care, healing, love and hope...
With love and light to you and yours....

Bizi

Epilogue-1

– Bijayalaxmi Nanda

Sometimes I wonder what is the purpose of bringing this collection together? Ruminations between two friends in making sense of the most confusing phase of contemporary times... Two cities in two corners of the world and two women divided in every way except for their binding friendship spanning childhood, youth and middle age. Two years have passed since we started writing and two years since the exploring of the possibility of putting it into print. Two years is a long time and one imagined that the book would become irrelevant. Dust would settle on the pandemic memories and not many would be able to understand the significance of being in a lockdown or wearing masks or running out of oxygen or the ambulance sirens renting the air. Some would remember and some would mourn the death of loved ones alone in hospital beds, the clamour for remisdivir, steroids and ivermectin and oxygen cylinders and hospital beds ... some hearts would be irretrievably broken but all will go on...

Yet the pandemic continues to ebb and flow and in regular intervals born again and christened like bald, hairless, wrinkled faced babies -delta and omicron each with a character, mind of its own. The N95 masks, vaccines and the sanitisers have settled to eternal discomfort on our skins like aging lines. No longer surreal or new normal ... like disagreeable family members who have now come to stay for eternity with us.

The collection of our emails floating on this turbulent ocean remains relevant for the times.

By publishing this book are we discussing the strength of bond of female friendships or a specific point about celebrating the female spirit of resilience? Instead of lapsing into a mire of devastating gloom and venting our woes through the letters we decided to make something concrete of it. This enterprising idea of a book. Was this kind of publishing venture unique to us? Did we know of other women who made something out of the ragged pieces of godforsaken lives in this period... Can we make a generic point about women's lives based on this narrative? There are women who discovered their latent talents of baking, cooking, painting, writing and music and strived to make something of it during this phase. Did other genders behave differently? Did they lack the much-needed positive energy? We must confess we really do not know that... All we know is that we are more alert to women's stories and understand it in in-depth ways and perhaps can say it better...

So, there are stories of bittersweet resilience that we bring to you about beautiful women who struggled to overcome the pandemic conditions and like the stitching the quintessential patchwork quilt they created a salvation for themselves and in the process for the world around them during this period.

Kamla Bhasin – the chronicle of a death celebrated (Thank you Marquez)

Kamla Bhasin was a well-known feminist, author and mobiliser of women's groups in India and across South Asia. Her authentic voice was drawn from her own experiences and negotiated through the women's movements that she was a part of. She was Kamladi (elder sister) to all who knew her and everyone felt she belonged to them in every way. Her natural child like demeanour, her sense of fun and humour, her emotive connections and her absolute delight in singing and sloganeering made her immensely accessible to all concerned. But this is not about a story about her life but about her death. In 2021 in the midst of this pandemic Kamladi who was in her most active activist phase online was diagnosed with terminal liver cancer. The doctors gave her a death sentence in their God like announcement. Three months of breathing, heaving life was all that was left... It was not as if this dreaded news did not hit her with the requisite shock that it was supposed to bring, it was not as if she did not desire to live for her son for whom she was a caregiver, it was not as if she did not try everything possible to find a way out.... But in the midst of it all she triumphed by her vulnerability – she reached out to her friends, created a support system around herself, visited hospitals for chemotherapy and tried alternative modes too of treatment. Prayers from all spiritual waves resounded around her. Her carefree spirit and her independent will, her ability to invoke co-dependence, security and love all coalesced to create the most beautiful song of female solidarity and friendship. The women around her were from all classes and communities and not necessarily from one ideology. But their love for her united them. She died soaked in this expansive love singing songs till the end ... a beautiful funeral of fragrant roses and jasmines and rhythmic songs....

Her celebrated will gave away her substantial wealth to the people of the movement except for the adequate part that she set aside for her son and his care givers. The pandemic had revealed the absolute isolation of people in their last moments making the possibility of saying a final goodbye more and more difficult. While some of that isolation was warranted to prevent transmission, some of it came from a baser human instinct not to move beyond one's comfort zone and reflected in selfish and egoistical tendency for most of us.

Kamladi of course was one for protocols for Covid prevention. Her son who was wheel-chair bound since childhood and needed 24-hour caregiving required protection. She also saw to it that no else was vulnerable to getting the virus while visiting her. She was herself tested on a regular basis and friends who visited or stayed with her ensured they were vaccinated and free from Covid. Yet in the midst of all this she was able to prove that ultimately the human spirit is capable of great love and compassion. We are ready to go beyond our selfish instincts to be there for each other, to celebrate each other and to laugh and sing and mourn and cry and remember and forget. It is a simple thought yet it is radical and transformational in every way. Only Kamala Bhasin was capable of revealing such a path to us... The path of human vulnerability, love, empathy and peace in life and death and beyond...

Rakhee Bakshee – Antifragile – Gaining from Disorder (Thank you Taleb)

Rakhee's story is the story of the everyday aspirational woman striving to stay afloat in a freelancing world. She has been in important positions both as a media consultant and an anchor with the Parliament and Indian Television for two decades. She was also the editor of the Women's Feature Services. Just before the pandemic Rakhee's work came to a standstill. The programme she was anchoring with Television came to an end, Women's Feature Services ended the contract with her and she was left in a precarious situation as far as her career was concerned. She kept dabbling with new ventures but reinventing yourself after an established career in television and other public forums especially in a senior position requires grit and determination. It also requires vibrant energy and positive strength. During the pandemic lockdown Rakhee launched an online platform titled Her-World India, initiated a blog on women's issues and held weekly talk shows online on the Zoom platform and later on YouTube speaking to experts on issues concerning the pandemic, women's health, online education and mental health. She celebrated women leaders across the country and brought in musicians, singers and poems to the platform bringing in a sense of hope and healing to the participants who watched her show. Her show was sustained through her own efforts without major financial assistance or technical know-how but that did not deter her from emphasising on quality. Today the experience with her platform led to the IIT and the Indian Institute of Public Administration reach out to her to engage her services for the organisation as a media consultant. She is anti-fragile in every sense. Every obstacle she faced she learnt from it and strived to adapt to the changing times by innovation and gaining from disorder.

Nupur Ray – Inheritance of loss yet eternal love (Thank you Kiran Desai)

Nupur lost her mother to the covid 19 in a quick two weeks ... there was no preparation, no understanding of how and why it happened. Her mother was in the middle of hustling, bustling life, a matriarch who had single-handedly taken care of all her three children and was now ruling with a golden hand spreading love, stories and doses of sound advice to her grandchildren. She was relatively young at 60 plus and was busy organising the wedding of her beloved younger son. She was the one to instruct, order and decide and her little army of sons, son-in-law, daughter and daughter-in-law carried it out. Her death was incomprehensible for them for she had not told them the plan for the future in so many words. Nupur suddenly found herself in the unenviable position of taking life forward as her mother meant for all of them. She was inconsolable. Her grief had paralysed her. Yet one day she shook up the gloom and in between her tears and fears strived to imagine what her mother would have wanted in that moment. She then painstakingly opened her mind to the planning of the wedding of her brother. The gloom and the doom notwithstanding, Nupur wove a beautiful tapestry of silk, golden, dreams and memories for the small and select wedding. She organised each programme of the wedding with the thought of her mother's wish and with her brother, sister-in-law and spouse let life come full circle in every way. Her mother became a living presence at the wedding in the ever-sparkling love between siblings and their spouses. The covid lockdown and protocol made it difficult. But she carried on with confidence driven by an indomitable will. It is the ultimate triumph of human spirit to be joyous and strive to complete responsibilities when one is hit with the hardest blows of one's life. Losing a mother for a daughter is like losing a part of the tapestry of one's being. Nupur sewed the tapestry gently yet powerfully to sustain the legacy of her mother. That is what women do ... that is what daughters do ... beautifully. powerfully ... amidst tears and fears ... yet rising above it all....

So let us all rise to find our feet in the shifting sands of time ... let us celebrate our women friends, let us amplify their voices, let us be their cheerleaders.

This book of emails/letters is a recognition of how love, loss and longing are not solely located in the realm of romantic and intimate relationships. Friendships are also the terrain which we navigate in order to survive, build and energise ourselves during our transformative and mundane moments. Finding that one friend who forgives you your silences and accepts you unconditionally is the greatest treasure one can ask for....

Find me
When I bury myself
In the silence of the desert
Under the blanket of unruly winter
Blisters on my non-descript lips
Calluses on my limping feet
Yet sparks of scalding hope
Will keep alive my scarred, shining soul.

Bijayalaxmi Nanda

Epilogue-2

– Sangita Misra

A year has flown by. It was March 12, 2020 , when the World Health Organization announced COVID-19 to be a pandemic.

The pandemic is still creating a pandemonium irrespective of masking, double masking, washing hands. A second wave has started in many countries around the world, and we are now being administered vaccines to safeguard our health, and the health of others. We still are carriers even though we have temporarily shielded ourselves from the threat of death. They say we are covered 95% ; they also say by July 2021, your part of the world would have vaccinated enough people to equal the entire population of the USA!

Here I am a first responder and have gotten the Moderna vaccine already. So also my husband, who got the Pfizer. A year has brought about many changes in the way we think and feel. But one thing has remained pure and untouched – our friendship. It has stood the test of time. A virus that turned out to be destructive to many, brought us together yet again. I guess women friendships are all about that; like the wedding vow in the Christian world "I Sangita Misra take you to be my friend, to have to hold from this day forward, for better, for worse, for richer, for poorer, in sickness and in health, to love and to cherish, till death do us do part."

Appendix

Recipes of Loss and Love

1. Dahi Bhata (Curd Rice)

Ingredients:

- 1 cup rice
- 2 cups water
- 2 cups curd
- Half teaspoon mustard seeds
- Half teaspoon cumin seeds
- 1 teaspoon urad dal
- 1 teaspoon chana dal
- 1/2 teaspoon grated ginger
- 6 to 7 curry leaves
- Salt to taste
- 1 teaspoon mustard oil

Preparation:

1. Pressure cook rice with water. Add curd to it once done. Cook on low heat. Add salt to taste. Set aside.
2. Heat oil in a pan. Add mustard seeds, cumin seeds, ginger, and curry leaves until they sputter. Add urad dal and fry until golden brown.
3. Add the seasoning to the curd rice that is set aside.
4. Serve with mango pickles and papad.

2. Ghuguni (Yellow Peas Curry)

Ingredients:

- 1 cup yellow peas
- 1 cup cubed potatoes
- 1 tablespoon garlic ginger paste
- 2 onions, sliced
- 1 tomato, sliced
- 1 tablespoon refined oil
- 2 bay leaves
- 1 teaspoon cumin seeds
- Garam masala, coriander powder, salt to taste

Preparation:

1. Boil peas and potatoes. Set aside.
2. Heat oil in a pan, add cumin/jeera seeds, bay leaves until they sputter. Add sliced onions and fry until they change color. Add garlic ginger paste.
3. Add turmeric and cook until oil separates. Add tomatoes until soft. Add one cup water, peas, and potatoes. Adjust consistency. Cook for 2 minutes.
4. Add garam masala and coriander leaves. Serve with Samosa/Bara or Puri/Paratha and pickle.

3. Tomato Khatta (Chutney)

Ingredients:

- 5 small tomatoes
- 1/2 teaspoon panch poron
- 10 raisins, 8 dates

- 200 grams jaggery
- 1/2 teaspoon cumin powder
- 1/2 teaspoon diced ginger
- 10 to 15 curry leaves
- 2 tablespoons refined oil

Preparation:

1. Heat oil in a pan. Add cumin seeds, panch poron, diced ginger, curry leaves and sauté until they sputter.
2. Add sliced tomatoes, turmeric, and salt. Cook until mushy. Add jaggery and stir over low heat.
3. Add dates and raisins, stir until sticky. Serve with steamed rice, dal, fried spinach, and potatoes.

4. Aloo Chakta (Mashed Potatoes)

Ingredients:

- 5 potatoes
- 1 onion
- 1 tablespoon mustard oil
- 1 teaspoon mustard and cumin seeds
- 1 green chili, 1 dry red chili
- Salt to taste

Preparation:

1. Pressure cook the potatoes. Peel and mash them.
2. Heat mustard oil in a pan, add cumin and mustard seeds until they sputter. Add green chilis, red chili, sliced onions and sauté until they change color.
3. Add the mashed potatoes and salt. Serve with steamed rice and dalma.

5. Dalma (Dal Cooked with Vegetables)

Ingredients:

- 1 cup arhar dal
- 2 carrots, 2 potatoes
- 1/2 cup cauliflower florets
- 1 raw banana, 2 eggplants
- 1/2 diced pumpkin
- 2 onions, 1 tomato
- 1 tablespoon ginger garlic paste
- 1 tablespoon refined oil
- 1 teaspoon turmeric powder, cumin powder
- Dry red chili, cumin and mustard seeds, bay leaf

Preparation:

1. Roast dal in a heated pressure cooker for 1 minute.
2. Add cut vegetables, bay leaf, turmeric, salt, and 3.5 cups of water. Pressure cook for two whistles and simmer for a couple of minutes.
3. In a pan, sauté onions until they change color. Add ginger garlic paste and cook until separated. Cook tomatoes until mushy.
4. Add the cooked paste to the dal and vegetables. Heat ghee separately, add cumin seeds, panch poron, and mustard seeds. Add to the cooked dal. Roast cumin and dry red chilis, grind to powder and sprinkle on the dalma. Serve with rice, aloo chakta, tomato khatta, mango pickles, and papad.

6. Aloo Dum (Fried Potatoes in Spicy Curry)

Ingredients:

- 4 medium potatoes
- 3 tablespoons vegetable oil

- 2 tablespoons plain yogurt
- 1/2 teaspoon ginger/garlic paste
- 3 teaspoons finely chopped onions
- 1/2 teaspoon cayenne powder
- 1/2 teaspoon coriander powder
- 3 cloves
- 1 bay leaf
- 1 cardamom
- 1 teaspoon Garam Masala

Preparation:

1. Boil potatoes with skin on. Peel and cube them into medium chunks.
2. Heat 2 tablespoons oil in a wok. Fry cubed potatoes until golden brown. Remove and set aside.
3. In the same pan, add bay leaf, cumin seeds, cloves, cardamom. Sauté for a few seconds.
4. Add ginger garlic/sliced onion and fry on slow heat.
5. Add spice powders and yogurt mix, cook until oil separates.
6. Add potatoes and fry for 2 minutes. Add 2 cups water and bring to a boil.
7. Simmer low for 7 minutes. Add garam masala, stir. Serve warm over dahi bara.

7. Dahi Bara (Lentil Fritters Soaked in Curd)

Ingredients:

- 1 cup Urad Dal
- 2 cups plain yogurt

- 2 cups cold water
- 2 cups warm water to soak the dumplings
- Oil for deep frying
- 2 tablespoons cumin seeds
- 3 whole dried red chili

Preparation:

1. Soak 1 cup urad dal overnight until it swells up.
2. Grind to a fine paste in a grinder with a little water.
3. Fluff the batter using your hands for 5 to 10 minutes to incorporate air.
4. Whisk 2 cups plain yogurt with 2 cups cold water to thin buttermilk consistency.
5. Heat vegetable oil for deep frying. Wet your hands, take 1 tablespoon of batter, make a hole with your thumb, and gently slide it into the oil. Repeat and fry until lightly brown on both sides.
6. Drain the baras, soak them in a big bowl of warm water for 2-3 minutes.
7. Gently squeeze the water from the baras, making sure they do not break. Slide them into the whisked yogurt/water mix.
8. Dry roast 2 tablespoons cumin seeds and 3 whole dried red chili until they give off a nutty aroma. Dry grind and add 1 tablespoon salt. Mix and store in an airtight container.
9. Take the lentil dumplings infused with yogurt sauce in a bowl. Sprinkle with jeera/lanka gunda (dry roasted cumin/red chili powder) mixed with salt. Enjoy with or without Aloo Dum.

8. Papri Chaat (Fried Crispies)

Ingredients:

- 1 can of chickpeas, rinsed well
- 2 dahi baras with yogurt sauce
- 3 pieces of aloo dum with gravy
- Coriander chutney
- Tamarind chutney
- Chili garlic sauce
- Your favorite mixture
- Cubed onions and cilantro leaves for garnish.

Preparation:

1. Place all ingredients in a bowl.
2. Toss them together.

9. Gajja (Flour Crispies)

Ingredients:

- All-purpose flour/Maida- 1 cup
- Atta/whole wheat flour- 1/2 cup
- Desi Ghee/melted butter - 1/4th cup
- Curd - 2 tablespoons
- Soda - 1/4 tsp
- Saunf/fennel seeds- 1 tablespoon
- Vegetable oil- to deep fry
- Salt, a pinch

Method:

1. Mix flour, saunf, baking soda, yogurt, and ghee until it forms a crumbly structure.
2. Add water and knead to a smooth dough.
3. Make medium-sized balls and roll into a thick circle using a rolling pin.
4. Cut vertically into long strips, then cut horizontally and remove the strips.
5. In a deep wok, add enough oil to fry. Deep fry the cut strips.

Enjoy your delicious dishes!